The New Editorial Team

By The God Editor of Doom

When I started **Phenomenal Stories** magazine in late August 2018, it was largely a solo project from an editing perspective, but that said, I had a lot of help and a lot of encouragement from those around me.

Photo by Gary W. Ziroli

Those folks included, of course, my wife, Carole A. Tomlinson, as well as Richard H. Nilsen, J.D. Hayes-Canell, Gary W. Ziroli and others.

I'd been an editor for what seems more than three or four lifetimes, so editing the magazine came relatively naturally to me, but other aspects were far more challenging. My biggest worry was coming up with cover art for every issue. I'm a photographer, but otherwise not really a visual artist. I can't paint or draw or sculpt, etc., so I really needed to be able to rely upon actual artists to help me.

The first two issues were reasonably easy because Richard H. Nilsen's daughter, Cara Nilsen, is an established artist and art teacher. She had, a few years back, done some black and white drawings for a story titled "Cara's Party." Since I wanted to run this story in the first issue — well, OK, I wanted to run the first in the series, "Dali's Deck," but I had no illustrations for it — I took the drawing of Faun reading the Tarot. I spent a bit of time trying to color it, not really knowing what I was doing. I showed it to Carole, an accomplished and registered artist, who said it was OK.

So, I had my first cover. Using another drawing from "Cara's Party," I set about making that color as well. I knew a little bit more by then, so it went a little easier. Then the third cover came up, for the November 2018 issue, and I was lost. There were no more illustrations available for me to colorize or use. I had been taking some photos of bees flying at flowers recently, and that gave me an idea. I took one of those flower photos, stylized, gave it a sort of desert background and then put a bunch of bees and space ships zooming in to the flower. I wasn't sure about it, but Carole and Gary liked it, so even if they were trying to placate me, I got the confidence to use it.

Then Savn C. Crishnan happened along, thankfully, and he took over doing many of the covers for the magazines. Mercifully. Gary was willing to pitch in with some of his great art for some covers, largely with the advent of the second magazine to the roster, **Phenomenal Stories Quarterly**. If I get an idea for a cover, I'll do one sometimes, but generally, I'll pass along such ideas to Savn. He'll huff, sigh and go away only to return a cover better than I could expect.

Certainly the nature of the writing requires, well, writers, and I was lucky enough to know some good ones before I started the magazines. They've made all of the magazines what they are.

I said there "started the magazines," and that's really the point of this piece, rather than me just whining about not having sufficient talent to create all the covers myself.

J.D. Hayes-Canell, long ago, once called me "Cecil B. De Tomlinson" because I tend to think in big, epic things, like the famed Hollywood mogul, Cecil B. De Mille. Can't say Jeff's wrong, although that epic thing has gotten me in trouble, and often.

When it came to the magazines... hmm... well, a bit more history.

I started my first magazine, a literary small press one titled **The Antediluvian Levee** way, way back in 1986. It was a time when I and those around me got in heavily with the small press crowd. We re-awakened Zirlinson Publishing — which we'd started in 1983 — the year before and produced a lot of chapbooks, all by me, sad to say. We kind of were burnt out on those by 1986, but we'd had a lot of dealings with Joseph Bruchac and his small press empire, and that led inevitably to the creation of our first magazine.

So, somewhere in 1986, Eileen Anderson — a co-founder of Zirlinson — and Michael P. Easterly and I all started working on **The Antediluvian Levee**. We'd put the word out that we were looking for submissions and get lots of them. The great thing about that was that we got to pick the very best stuff from the bunch. For that reason, I think **The Antediluvian Levee** holds up very well all these years later.

We didn't do a second issue, which we should have. We had enough strong material left over from the first issue that a second one would have been at least as good. Not sure why we didn't do it, but we didn't.

Three years later, I got the idea to do a role-playing game magazine on an odd format. In those days before desktop publishing was readily available for poor publishers, the way we made chapbooks was to turn a standard sized — 8.5x11-inch — piece of paper sideways in the [shudder] typewriter. For each sheet of paper, we got four pages, each 5.5x8.5 inches. So, what I did for this new magazine was put the sheet of paper in the correct way, but cut it in half to still get four pages per sheet. The dimensions, though, were 4.25x11 inches. I only ever saw one other magazine done this way years later. It was a speculative fiction magazine with a slicker cover than we could afford.

Our magazine, titled **The Game's Afoot**, lasted for 10 issues from 1989 to 1992. It had some success in California — where I had moved — reaching a circulation of around 200, not a bad number for a small press magazine with virtually no budget, no promotion.

After I started **The Game's Afoot**, I edited what started out as a one-off anthology, turned into a literary magazine, but ended up back as an anthology. I still consider it a magazine, though. It was titled **Different Deaths** and published only poetry, like **The Antediluvian Levee**.

Later on, 1996 I think, or 1997, I started yet another magazine that was supposed to have four issues per year, but ended up with only the first issue. It was called **Ride of the Horsemen** and consisted largely of columns, a little fiction, etc. It looked good and come together relatively easily. It's where the title God Emperor of Doom originated. J.D. Hayes-Canell at the time had never written for a magazine previously and, I guess, found working for an editor — me — to be a bit overwhelming. Not sure exactly, but he's the one who called me the GEOD.

Then, a decade later, I was starting a magazine to be called **Lost Carcosa**. I was doing the designs, getting the world out I was looking for material, was scheduled to do some introductory talks about it, etc. It never was published, though. A lot of other stuff got in the way. About all that remains is the cover and a couple of fiction pieces left unfinished. One of those, by me, actually is pretty good and I may finish it one day.

I retired from newspapers in 2009 and set out to be a photographer, but before long, was writing books. A lot of books. And editing, designing and publishing books for other writers.

Toward the end of the busiest year in the 35-year history of Zirlinson Publishing — 2018 — I revived the idea of doing a speculative fiction magazine. It seemed futile at first, but I pushed myself into it quickly and in less than a month, the first issue was in print.

Since **Phenomenal Stories** is a tribute to the pulp magazines — which I've collected and read for many years — I got thinking about the variations within the pulps in the prime era in which they were published, say 1923 to 1955 or so.

Hugo Gernsback, who created the first magazine solely dedicated to science fiction — which he called scientifiction — **Amazing Stories**, wanted to continually expand his publishing empire,

Richard H. Nilsen
Editor
Phenomenal Stories Quarterly

J.D. Hayes-Canell
Editor
Lost Carcosa Magazine

Delia McTavish
Editor
Phenomenal Novels Magazine

Bridget Flynn-O'Leary
Editor
Phenomenal Fiction Magazine

so within a year of his first issue of **AMZ** published **Amazing Stories Annual**. It became especially collectable because it's the first appearance of the complete novel, *Mastermind of Mars*, by Edgar Rice Burroughs. That magazine made money, so in 1928, Gernsback launched **Amazing Stories Quarterly**. When he was forced out of his own company, he almost immediately launched **Science Wonder Stories** and **Air Wonder Stories**, and not that long afterward, **Science Wonder Quarterly**.

Gernsback's quarterlies had new material in them, but a later incarnation of the quarterlies, under editor Ray Palmer, did this thing that could bring in more money without spending much. What Palmer did was take all the returned/unsold copies of the monthly **Amazing Stories**, rip the covers off and bind them into enormous magazines. Each issue of these **Amazing Stories Quarterly** had the previous three months of issues bound together.

While we don't expect any income from it, we're basically doing the same thing. The idea for **Phenomenal Stories Quarterly**, though, is just to have three issues of **Phenomenal Stories** bound together for easier reading and collecting. Despite the high cover price, **PSQ** is cheaper than buying each issue separately.

So, OK, I had **Phenomenal Stories** and **Phenomenal Stories Quarterly**, with the second taking only a little bit more work to put together. I already had the contents, so it was just a matter of creating the new issues with them.

Now, most editors would have been satisfied with that arrangement. Aside from the two magazines — one monthly, the other every three months — I still was writing my own books, taking photos every day and dealing with quite a number of personal/health crises. I should have been satisfied.

But, hey, if there was going to be a monthly speculative fiction magazine, there really should be a year-end "best of" magazine, too. And the title **Lost Carcosa** was just floating out there... so, I did the annual **Lost Carcosa** and released it before the end of 2018.

Hang on, though...

Since I am a photographer, and I know photographers, I started thinking about doing a photography magazine. And so, I asked three photographers I knew to give me their best work for what became **Images Magazine**. Just after it went to print, one of those photographers wanter her work removed for some religious reasons I still don't understand, which is why the Spring 2019 issue of **Images** is only 66 pages and has galleries by only three photographers.

Still not enough, though.

I started thinking about taking the novels that we serialize in **Phenomenal Stories**, and fitting the pieces back together. With a nod to **Fantastic Novels Magazine** and Editor Mary Gnaedinger, we launched Phenomenal Novels Magazine in July 2019.

And finally, in August 2019, we launched **Phenomenal Fiction Magazine**, collecting the short fiction from **Phenomenal Stories**. Although, under editor Bridget Flynn-O'Leary, we will be including original fiction in **PFM**, too.

Bringing up Bridget, well that's where we're going next.

With all these magazines to edit, I finally decided I needed a little help, so I kicked myself upstairs with the new title of executive editor, overseeing all the magazine. OK, that's what I've been doing, but now I'm getting some day to day help by turning over some of the magazines to other editors.

One of ours staunchest allies and frequent contributors, Richard H. Nilsen took over the job of editor of **Phenomenal Stories Quarterly** as of the Autumn 2019 issue. Along with editing and assembling each issue, Richard will be assigning, selecting and maybe occasionally writing some new pieces that will be included in PSQ as bonus features.

J.D. Hayes-Canell is writing frantically these days, keeping us up on the adventures of his alter ego, Intrepid Reporter, in his column, as well as creating a lot of new fiction. With all that in mind, he still agreed to carve out some time to take the helm of **Lost Carcosa** magazine. He'll be working each year to gather the best of the magazines to then

assemble the year-end periodical.

Delia McTavish has written a few pieces for **Phenomenal Stories** and will be contributing interviews and other material to future issues. She's also agreed to take the reins at **Phenomenal Novels Magazine**, re-editing the previously serialized novels, writing editorials and bonus features, and, eventually we hope, selecting original, non-serialized novels for inclusion in the magazine.

Shawn M. Tomlinson
Executive Editor,
Editor
Phenomenal Stories,
Images Magazine

Finally we come back to Bridget Flynn-O'Leary, who's young and energetic and never seems to tire. She's taken over the newest of our magazines, **Phenomenal Fiction**, as of the December 2019 issue. Although **PFM** right now is a three times a year collection of short fiction from **Phenomenal Stories**, Bridget is enthusiastically pursuing previously unpublished stories. She hopes to take **PFM** first to quarterly, then to bimonthly and possibly to monthly publication, if she can get enough stories to justify it.

As I've written before, we're not all that concerned with making money with these magazines, which sets us apart from most publishers. We're mainly concerned with producing magazines that are enjoyable to read and fun to collect.

That's what every person on the new editorial team is working toward.

Aside from overseeing all the magazines, I'll still be directly editing **Phenomenal Stories** and **Images Magazine**.

So, welcome, please

• Richard H. Nilsen, editor, **Phenomenal Stories Quarterly**

• J.D. Hayes-Canell, editor, **Lost Carcosa**

• Delia McTavish, editor, **Phenomenal Novels Magazine**

• Bridget Flynn-O'Leary, editor, **Phenomenal Fiction Magazine**

We're set... as long as I don't get any crazy ideas for even more magazines...

— ***The Editor***

ZIRL & SONS PUBLISHERS

The Horror at the Canal

By Cú Chulainn Cavannaugh

I

There was no time to run.

The thing looked up at me from a hole in the dense, green water.

I stood powerless, motionless on the liftbridge.

There was nothing I could have done.

From the abyss, a ladder formed, slippery, slimy green, like the water.

The thing underneath smiled its other worldly smile and invited me in. It was an invitation every part of my brain and soul told me to reject, yet I found myself climbing down the ladder, slipping beneath the still water of the canal.

The thing didn't touch me. It didn't make a sound. It just watched me as I climbed down.

Forever I climbed. Forever and it never changed, except that the liftbridge above me grew smaller, smaller and finally was gone.

I stood silent on the cave floor. The ladder was gone, so was the hideous thing.

Around me were hundreds, perhaps thousands, of tortured, dirty people, chained and piling rocks. There were fires and horrid smells belching with acrid smoke from the floor and walls.

In front of me was some obscene altar. Around it stood five creatures covered in deep black robes.

I walked toward them, slowly, but purposefully.

When I was face to face with them, with the inhuman face etched in bloody stone above and behind the altar, I opened my shirt and waited.

The tallest of the priests took the tiny, ravenous beast from its cage and brought it to my chest.

With razor-sharp teeth, the tiny beast chewed in a frenzy through my flesh, through my bones and to my heart.

The priests began their incantations and the giant form of the ancient god formed above the altar. It laughed, ripped the heads from its priests and devoured me whole.

I woke with the same frantic, sweaty fear I do every night. Every night, I have the same dream, the same nightmare vision.

Every night I feel those razor teeth tear into me, feel all the pain, except I can't ever seem to die because I know, I know I will wake again each day to find that I am whole again.

Psychiatrists can't help me. They can't find a reason for the dreams.

II

"Mr. Maxwell, I'm sorry to have two bits of bad news for you, but I do," Dr. Kimball said. "But perhaps, in the long-term, it will help. First, we can find no direct connection between anything in your life to these nightmares. As you know, we've tried switching food many times, switching what you drink, what you take in in any way. We've changed and stopped medications, and tried experimental drugs.

"I'm afraid to say we really have found nothing, nor has anything we've done seemed to help. The good news is, we have a specialist, doctor from London, who may be able to help you. She has done some amazing work with schizophrenics and people with other types of mental issues. Her name is Dr. Hieronymus and she will be here in a day or two."

I stared at Kimball as he talked nervously, keeping a distance from me. He always kept a good distance, and he always looked like he was about to run, which I suppose, he was.

He was a big Rock Slabjaw type guy, chiseled features, perfectly groomed couple a days growth of beard. He was the type women fell for instantly. As doctors go, though, he wasn't particularly bright and he probably got me as a patient because his superiors knew there was nothing that could be done for me. I could see from the moment I met him that he didn't argue against taking my case because he wanted to sleep with my wife. Well, good luck to him, but it wasn't going to help me escape my horror.

As calmly as I could, I said, "You said there were two bits of bad news."

"What?" Kimball said, inching back toward the door. "Oh, sorry, yes. Your wife, who has authority

over you in your current state, has signed papers to keep you here indefinitely."

"Is she here to visit?" I asked, still very, very calm.

"Ah, no, no she isn't," Kimball said, avoiding my eyes.

He was nailing my wife. I could see that in the way he acted. One more reason he wanted to keep his distance.

Not sure why.

Everybody screws my wife. I think she even had a brief affair during our honeymoon. I expect her to have her legs apart most of the time for other men.

This Dr. Kimball was good looking, probably, and he was big. She's small and likes big men dominating her. It amuses her because she's always really the one in control, and making big, stupid guys like Kimball here think he was in power as he sent her into screaming fits of joy. I'm not a big, stupid guy... OK, well, I'm not a big guy... It wasn't physical power she wanted from me, but power over the family heritage.

Looks like she's got that now... she may run into a formidable foe, though, when/if my sister comes out of hiding... I'd almost like to see that... except then my sister would rip me up and apart for letting my wife anywhere near the family heritage. Then, if my brother... no... he'll have nothing to say... not after he did almost this same thing.

What is it about Maxwell men the women they want?

Both me and my brother ... hardly ever talking to each other... both had been sans female companionship for nearly half a decade, then suddenly got "found" by some beautiful, intelligent, well, brilliant woman with intense interest in the other worldly.

Sad eyes.

Sad effing eyes.

They always get me in trouble, my brother, too.

Our instincts tell us to help women with sad eyes.

So, we fall in love with them.

I know no male member of our family, our ancient and still strong family, who hasn't fallen to the same trap. That's a lot a guys, too, including cousins, nephews, etc.

We're all the bloody same!

We fall for those horrid, beautiful, sad eyes...

We only marry those with brains, too, all of us, and that's really what gets us in trouble....

If only we could live with stupid, beautiful women, perhaps our lives would be better, like most people's lives. Stupid men get taken in by smart women and vice versa.

Not us.

We always, always have to have women as smart or smarter than us just to remain interested at least long enough to say "I do."

And then the trouble really begins...

My wife's easy... in more ways than one ... she just wants money, property and power. Human, normal power. The power to hire and fire, get what she wants. My brother's wife... she's something else. Wants power on several different

levels, including power beyond this world.

She's not my problem.

My wife really isn't anymore, either. Now that she's had me committed, well, she'll not need to have anything else to do with me. She'll make sure there's lots of money to keep me here, but other than that, she'll be screwing and spending and making and breaking politicians from here to the end of her life. Or, well, until my sister gets ahold of her.

In my thoughts, I'd forgotten Kimball still was there. He was pretending to keep going over my chart as I looked up.

"You may want to get as many screws as possible with my wife, Dr. Kimball," I said. "As fast as you can. You'll be replaced quickly."

"What?" Kimball stammered. "I'm not... having sex with your... wife!"

"Sure ya are," I said. "Everybody does. You probably had to take a number. Like I said, though, the guy with the next number is queuing up right now, so nail her as much as you can before she yells next."

"I think it's time for your meds, Mr. Maxwell," Kimball said. "I'll send in Betsy. She'll give them to you. Good day, Mr. Maxwell."

I think I may have pissed him off, but it doesn't matter. He's not helping me, just helping himself to my "bury me in a Y-shaped coffin" wife, as Black Adder said.

III

He was gone. Nothing to do but wait for my nurse. That would be fun. Or not. Depended upon who she brought with her.

I looked out the window. The facility I was in had a view of the Erie Canal, in fact, it was near the aqueduct that carried the canal over the road, Culvert Road, Route 33.

That actually, probably, was the safest part of the canal because the water had to be shallow to go over the aqueduct. It was when it got deep on either side of the aqueduct that it scared me. It probably would be better if this nuthouse was somewhere else.

It wasn't, and that had to do with my wife and her nastiness. She knew the nightmare had to do with the canal because I'd been foolish enough to tell her about the dream.

It wasn't long afterward that I was in here.

I didn't realize just how vicious she was until I woke up in here.

Funny, I guess. Especially since we live far south of here at Lily Dale, near my brother's estate.

In case you never heard of it, Lily Dale is a run down psychic hot point. It was founded in the 19th century, I think, by a couple of scamming sisters who kind of sparked off the whole spiritualism craze. Harry Houdini spent a lot of his later life debunking the spiritualists and their seances.

My other brother, Robert, bought a couple of houses there when he first was going to get married to his harpy wife. They used the house directly on Cassadaga

Lake as their house, the other one — they called it "The Lab" — as a library and research center. A lot of bad, bad books in The Lab and Robert probably read them all. Explains partially at least what happened to the poor bastard before he disappeared.

When I got married, Robert already had acquired a bunch of houses at Lily Dale, which is a gated community. Not for rich people, but for "mediums" and the like. Nice to be a rich author and lecturer. Not that the rest of us are poor, but Robert tends to spend money rather than sit on it. We, most of us, sit on it.

Anyway, he gave me and my bride a house five doors down from his with a great view of the lake. Ideal, for a time. Then I caught my wife doing two guys at once out on the back lawn and the fast hard slap of reality caught me hard in the face.

Our marriage was over, mostly, at that point, but a legal maneuver she'd made before the wedding kept us together. Otherwise, she'd have taken away every cent I had.

Told ya. She's smart. I'm stupid.

She made it clear she was going to screw anyone she wanted, but as a consolation prize — her actual words — she brought her younger sister to live with us and put us in bed together. Stupid thing was, I fell for her, for Kelly, damned fast. Unlike her sister, Kelly's actually a good person, a real human being.

And one day, Kelly was gone, sent off by Lucifer's trainer herself, my wife. Kelly basically was abducted, sent off where I couldn't find her. Wasn't long after that that the dream began to take me every night.

Since the dream is about the canal, she was willing to hurt me as much as possible by putting me in this facility right next to it, far from home. I guess she doesn't expect me to get better and that I'm gonna be in here until... until I'm dead, I guess.

I think I'll disappoint her. I intend to get out.

Betsy came in a few minutes later and I dreaded it. She was gorgeous, big breasts, wonderful lips that always made me think of things I shouldn't be thinking of. She was single. I could tell because she wore no ring and always had dresses and jeans at least two sizes too small for her. The scrub tops she wore also were too tight and gave a good view of her breasts.

All things that were pleasant enough to enjoy, except I couldn't because Betsy's the one who brought the drugs.

I tried to fight it, well, every day. The drugs seemed to make the nightmare worse than it'd been.

Betsy always persisted, though, sometimes with big guys holding me down until every pill and shot was given.

"Are we going to have trouble today?" she asked, grinning and practically shoving her cleavage in my face.

"No," I said. "I do wish someone would reconsider the drugs, though. Dr. Kimball — did you know he's banging my wife? — he

said the drugs weren't working, so why isn't he stopping them?"

I noted that she turned red when I mentioned Kimball and my wife. It went quickly from being embarrassed to being angry. Hmmm. Kimball had been banging Betsy, too, and she probably was in love with him and she just found out he had another lover.

Oh well.

To my astonishment, Betsy gave me a very intense look. She sent the big guys away, locked the door behind them. She set the pills and needles on a table, the practically ripped off her top. No bra there to contain my favorite things.

She grabbed me, pushed me back on my bed, put those astonishing and real breasts in my face. She had her skirt up, my underwear down... and I was inside her. She rode me hard, then rolled me on top of her.

Why not?

She always had me hard the moment she walked in, so why not a revenge screw? Not like I had a real wife to be faithful to, and the love of my life, Kelly, could be dead for all I knew.

Betsy wanted revenge on Dr. Slabjaw, so why not.

After a couple of goes, she fixed her clothes back to normal.

She leaned over to kiss me, said, "I'll be back tonight."

I thought for a moment she'd take pity on me since we'd had such a great time, but she caught sight of her drug kit, turned and got me to take all the pills, all the shots, without complaints.

It was around 1:30 p.m. when Betsy left.

I fought as long as I could, but the drugs put me to sleep...

IV

There was no time to run.

The thing looked up at me from a hole in the dense, green water....

I stood powerless, motionless on the lift-bridge.... Wait... something different... I could... move a little... that had never happened before. My hands worked, even if my arms and legs were not under my control... my hands were.

There was nothing I could have done. That still was true. I tried to move my body, tried to run, to change the nightmare even a little...

From the abyss, the ladder formed, slippery, slimy green, like the water and as the thing underneath smiled its other worldly smile, I began to climb. It was an invitation every part of my brain and soul told me to reject, yet I found myself climbing down the ladder, slipping beneath the still water of the canal.

The thing didn't touch me. It didn't make a sound. It just watched me as I climbed down. Forever I climbed, the only thing changing was the lift-bridge above me growing smaller, smaller and until finally, I stood on the cave floor, silently. The bridge, the ladder, the creature and the world above me, gone.

I was compelled, forced to climb down the ladder. But my hands

worked for me. I kept trying to think of something that I could do with my hands, but if I did anything different climbing down the ladder, I'd fall. Certain death, but would I wake up or really be dead? I waited, used my hands only as I was compelled to do.

Around me were hundreds, thousands, of tortured, dirty people, chained and piling rocks, for reasons I cannot comprehend. Some of them looked up at me, some with glimmers of hope, some with blank, already dead eyes. A naked woman covered in so much filth I barely could tell she was naked stared at me the longest, mouthed something to me, but I didn't understand her. So, using my working hands, I grabbed her by the waist and pulled her to me against her chains. I kissed her through the dirt, the grime, the blood, the gore.

She was astonished, and everything stopped for a second.

No one knew what to do.

Something was different and it threw off their compulsion or script or whatever.

Then everything started again, as if someone went from "pause" to "play" on some cosmic, other worldly remote control.

Then it was as it had been.

There was no way in or out of cave we were all desperately trapped in. There were fires and horrid smells belching with acrid smoke from the floor, a viscous substance oozing thickly from cracks in the wall, the strong taste of iron in the back of my throat telling me it was blood.

Was this hell? Is this the true Inferno we, as children, were threatened with for misbehaving? I quickly tried running through my head all the grievances I may have caused; my thoughts were coming up blank. I began to walk, against my will, to the back of the cave.

In front of me stood an altar, obscene, if there was ever a truer definition of the word, built from the walls of the cave. As I drew nearer, my feet with a mind of their own, I realized it was not made of wood and stone, but instead flesh and bones, stained red by the never end trickles dripping from the walls. In front of the alter were five creatures. I do not know if they are human or otherwise, covered in deep crimson, almost black, robes. I could barely make out the sounds of their chant over the echoes of breaking rocks, chains scraping the stone covered flooring, and screams of whips hitting backs.

I continued to walk toward them, slowly, but purposefully. Gracefully and effortlessly, they stood at the same time, parting slightly, leaving me in the middle to look up at the inhuman face etched in the bloody stone in the middle of the alter. Unlit candles began to spring to life and bringing forth dancing shadows across the already grotesque carving. On the alter was a bird cage, sitting inside of it quietly was a creature I've never seen before. The beast was quiet as one of the priests took it from its cage and carried it to me in both hands.

Stopping in front of me, the priest ran a finger down my shirt and I could feel the hair on my chest singe as my shirt fell open. I gritted my teeth from the pain of the heat as the creature jumped from the priests' hand and with razor-sharp teeth began to chew through my flesh and bones in a frenzy. I'm not sure which was louder, my screams or the incantations of the priests.

I tried to get my hands around the clawing beast, but my arms still were under the control of something else. I couldn't get my hands high enough. The pain was unbearable, but I forced myself to look down at the clawing, devouring beast for the first time. It looked up at me and I got a voice in my head, gruff, guttural, demonic.

It demanded: "Inside! Together we control! Inside"

I understood. As horrible as the scenario was, I looked at the beast, in its fire eyes, nodded. Suddenly, the pain stopped as I saw the beast's tiny tail slither inside my chest and the flesh healing and closing.

Feeling the beast's enormous brain in my head was overwhelming, but I forced myself to accept it.

The sounds around me came to a deafening halt as the ancient beast from above the altar came to life, filling the cave with laughter.

Tentacles slithered from the wall and through the altar, wrapping around each of the priest's necks. As the beast popped their heads off, it's laughing grew louder and the last thing I remember... No! The beast and I used enormous power, power we absorbed from all around and as the larger tentacled beast turned its attention to me, the part where it usually devoured me and I woke up, I gave it a thunderous command: "Bow down!" I said with ultimate confidence I'd never felt before.

Cthulhu Junior stopped. It looked way, way down at me. I thought our command didn't work. It shouldn't have worked.

It did work.

The tentacled beast stopped killing everyone, got down on its knees, still towering way over me, then bowed down in front of me, the horrible head coming to the floor before me.

My next move would have been to have the formerly stone demigod release the people, but...

I woke with the same frantic, sweaty fear I do every night. The same dream, the same nightmare vision.

Except this time, I had a raw feeling of extreme power. I didn't know if the beast really was inside my chest, or if I'd conquered the demi-god or what happened next, or if it was anywhere near as real as it all feels.

I stared at the dim insane asylum ceiling lights, orange, somehow slightly sinister.

The drugs were at that aphrodisiac point. Odd. Drugs to calm down a crazy, schizophrenic patient shouldn't give him a solid, constant erection for hours. Hard to ignore.

That night, I didn't have to. I

heard the key card in the door lock, then the loud click of the lock unlocking.

Betsy was back, voracious and determined. She knew what the drugs did to me and roughly when the effect she wanted would occur.

Like earlier that day, or was it yesterday, the red lights of the cameras went out and Betsy set her mind to giving her and me the most pleasure either of us could imagine.

V

It was evening and I was awake, but still groggy from the medications.

Betsy was gone, but probably back on duty, unless she took the day off to recover.

Much as I hate the drugs, gotta admit they got me to feel an intensity with Betsy I'd never felt before. I hoped she didn't tire of me soon.

The hazy part of the drugs was fading now, fast, and reality, horrible as it is, was setting in.

That's when *she* walked in.

She was beautiful in an ethereal sort of way, not blatant sex like Betsy. That ethereal feel to her made me want her terribly, yes sexually, but more than that.

She made me want a divorce, which I should have had long ago.

Her eyes... they were beautiful, but not sad. They were haunted a little, but who's aren't?

Despite the lack of sad eyes, I wanted her more than I'd ever wanted a woman. I wanted her to live a life with me, be with me always. I knew ... knew ... she would be loyal and kind and loving ... but best, an equal or even superior mind.

I knew her in that moment as if I'd known her a lifetime. She "felt" right, like so few people ever had, like no lover ever had, despite a lifetime of searching.

She smiled without it being one of those doctor patronizing smiles.

"Hello, Mr. Maxwell," she said. "I'm Dr. Jani Hieronymus and I'm here to..."

She hesitated, struggled for a minute, looked deeply into my eyes and I *knew*.

I *knew* it was her, the woman from the dream, the one who always tried to talk to me, the one I kissed. I *knew*.

She knew, too, I think, from the look on her face, but being a professional, a doctor, someone who deals with delusions every day, she quickly wrote off what she'd seen, pretended it never happened.

I sank back into myself a little.

Perhaps she was right to pretend it wasn't real. Nothing but pain and madness that way. I accepted it...

Then a guttural voice in my head said, "She it. Take her."

That wasn't going to happen.

"Take her! Yours! Ours!"

That last grimy scream in my head is what made me terrified the most.

"Ours?"

There was something... something really dangerous about me and Dr. Hieronymus even being in the same room together. I didn't

know what to do to save her, but I had to at all costs.

I had been sitting quietly, never making any attempt to harm anyone, attack anyone.

I grabbed a pen from the doctor's pocket and lunged for the big, meaty orderly at the door. He hardly saw it coming until I was at him.

I stabbed him several times in his chest, his arms. He screamed before he realized he could destroy me.

The beast inside me wanted the first stab to be through the eye, kill the guy instantly. It was all I could do to aim the pen elsewhere. I wasn't about to kill someone, no matter what the demon inside me told me to do.

They dragged me down, hit me with night sticks a lot. Dr. Hieronymus stabbed me with a needle and I started to fade.

"Run!" I told her weakly. "Get away from here. Run..."

There was no time to run.

The thing looked up at me from a hole in the dense, green water....

VI

They thought I was asleep, Kimball and Hieronymus, and they hadn't gotten to me yet. They were talking about something else.

"...three of them, three kids," Dr. H. was saying. "Dried up dead like mummies."

"It is weird," dumb Kimball said obviously. "No leads, of course. The police are baffled, but they're baffled by how corn flakes work."

I feigned sleep, mind racing through the drug haze. The thing in my chest was fighting me for control. It nullified the drugs, made me clear instantly, which was a mistake on its part.

It wanted Dr. Hieronymus. It wasn't gonna get her.

She and Kimball were just outside my door.

I noticed for the first time the restraints on my arms and legs. I snapped them with strength I shouldn't had, but the damned thing wanted Dr. Hieronymus badly and thought freeing me would get her.

No clothes. I'd been there too long and my lovely wife had made it permanent. No need for me to have clothes, they thought, so there were none.

Didn't matter.

The window glass that shouldn't have shattered did easily and I was outside.

Although the demon beast within helped me break out, it realized too late its mistake. Breaking out meant I wasn't getting Dr. Hieronymus for it. Instead, I raced across the parking lot, toward the looming canal beyond.

Only a vague sense of what I was doing was in my head. I could feel the creature starting to fight me hard. The pain seared through my chest, inside my body. I dropped to the hard pavement, yelling out before I could stop myself.

"Mr. Maxwell," someone screamed at me through the blinding pain.

I heard muffled footsteps running toward me, growing louder.

The creature ripped out of me chest. I saw it scurrying away, guttural curses cast around it.

I knew there should be a gaping hole in my chest that would kill me. Blood should have been gushing out.

It wasn't.

Betsy arrived that moment, bent down to me.

"Mr. Maxwell!" she said again. "What's wrong? You're covered in blood. What happened?"

Couldn't explain that.

"Leave me, Betsy, let me out of here," I said, struggling to stand.

"I'm not leaving you," she said. "I want to help you. I'll do anything."

"Get me away from here," I said. "The canal... it's calling to me. It wants me for something. Gotta get outta here or... or... we're all dead. I know you think I'm crazy... probably am... Dr. Hieronymus... it/they want her. Not gonna..."

I was standing, leaning heavily on my favorite nurse. She gave me a small, strained smile.

"You're not crazy," she said. "Come on. I'll take you to my place. It's safe there."

She helped me to her car and started to drive off the lot as we heard alarms sounding behind us.

They must have figured out I was gone. Bad PR to let crazy people loose on the neighbors. The were coming after me.

I still was weak from my struggles, kept fading in and out as she drove what seemed a long, long way.

Finally we stopped. She came around the car, opened the door and helped me out. She guided me with my arm around her to her door, then inside the old house, then directly to the bed.

Betsy tossed me down on the bed, went to a cedar chest near a window, unlocked it, then returned with a bottle of pills.

"These are all we need," she said, grinning at me.

She took one, then gave one to me.

She stripped my hospital clothes off, then stripped herself, went down on me enthusiastically. As she performed, the pill started to have its effect. I was hazy, but eternally erect, as long as the effect lasted.

Betsy mounted me, started riding me.

In the dim light, I saw it.

There was a jagged red line between her breasts, very recently closed. I could feel the creature inside her as I was inside her.

She rode me a long, long time before the pill made me fade out...

There was no time to run.

The thing looked up at me from a hole in the dense, green water....

Zirl & Sons Publishers

The Good Side To the Bad Seed

By Haldor R. Hallum

Seems like there used to be one in every family. When the country was dominated by agrarian families, it behooved every couple to produce as many children as possible.

Children made for cheap help on the farm.

Anyway, along with enough kids to produce a baseball team, there always seemed to be the hero child, forgotten child, spoiled prince or princess child and so on.

I'm not sure how all the designations get placed once you have 10 or 12 progeny, but whatever you want to categorize these family groupings, there always seemed to be at least one you could call the "bad seed."

Danny was the "bad seed" from our neighborhood.

He went through stages of badness.

From being the one who was always picking his nose in public to the one picking fights in the school yard, you could always count on Danny to take the heat off anything the rest of us might be up to.

The thing was, we just couldn't compete with his badness.

He'd out trump us every time.

That brings me to the cattle stealing thing.

This was in the Northeast so cattle rustling wasn't really a

thing.

But a local cattle auction had quite a few cattle going in and out until one Saturday night, the auction was a few short of a herd, so to speak.

It didn't take long for the local constabulary to fixate on Danny.

Why take the long way around and collect clues toward a finding that was a foregone conclusion?

Danny had already made a name for himself by this time and so he was the obvious focus of their attention.

The sheriff showed up at his family's barn and, sure enough, there were the missing cattle.

"And just what were you going to do with them?" I remember the deputy asking him.

The neighborhood had gathered at their farm to watch the fun.

It wasn't like he was fooling anyone or that anyone was surprised.

"Figured I'd cut 'em up and have vittles for the family all winter long," was Danny's reply.

I had to hand it to him.

Danny didn't dissemble a bit.

Straight out with it.

I didn't even have to be at his trial to hear him plead, "Guilty as charged."

Even the bad seed had a good side to him.

PHENOMENAL STORIES

ZIRL & SONS PUBLISHERS

God Editor of Doom's Note: Intrepid writer J.D. Hayes-Canell first introduced us to his fantasy world in the January 2019 issue of ***Phenomenal Stories*** *with the four-part serial,* **The Red Wizard**. *J.D.'s fantasy world is probably more akin to* **Deadwood** *than* **Harry Potter**; *a lot more grit and reality grip the reader here. Korvus, Nîlo and the rest are back for this installment, another four-part serial story we're proud to present here in the pages of* ***Phenomenal Stories*** *first. We look forward to the first full novel, hopefully to be published in our sister publication,* ***Phenomenal Novels Magazine*** *in the near future. In the meantime, please enjoy this third part of* **The Blue Wizard**.

The Blue Wizard

By J.D. Hayes-Canell

(Part 3 of 4)

The scrawny man scurried into a rickety dive along the water front. Here the reek of decay was almost carried off by the breeze from the Sybata sea. A snaggle toothed woman sat behind the bar, short and squat with a sallow look to her skin and a cast in one eye. A rat scuttled along the wall unnoticed by either of them.

"Well, if it ain't Stanbury th' Weasel, what brings yer sorry ass 'round 'ere?"

"Lookin' fer Chet, is 'e 'round?"

"In th' back room. Mind y' knock first!"

Stanbury scuttled through a filthy ragged curtain and down the

hall that stunk of piss and something fouler. He stopped at the door and as usual, had to suppress a shudder. The door didn't belong. It wasn't quite rectangular, but he couldn't say how. It wasn't made of any wood he'd ever seen, but it was grained; some of the knots in the graining looked like elongated faces shrieking in horror. There was no knob, just a finger wide slot, big enough for three fingers, lined with a slick metal.

With trembling hand, Stanbury lightly rapped at the door. There came a hissing sound, and the stench around him grew thicker. Tendrils of a yellowish fog seeped up from the floor and caressed him in a horrid clammy way that made his soul want to retch.

The door opened silently on a darkened room. The only light came from a single pinkish candle burning atop a human skull, still red and dripping.

The blood from the skull slid up into the base of the candle, slowly turning it from pink to red.

Beside the table where the skull rested was a single chair, cold, metal shaped like a bat with writhing tentacles where it's mouth should be.

Shaking with mortal fear, Stanbury approached it and waited.

From within the darkness a voice, oily and redolent with harsh screaming death spoke.

"Sit. Speak."

Almost beyond hope of surviving, Stanbury sat. Instantly his limbs became paralyzed and icy fingers stole into his brain.

"I've come m'lord t' tell you 'bout the strangers." He grimaced, revolted by the alien groping in his mind.

"I've sensed them. What do you know?"

"Two days ago they showed up at the Grim Gargoyle an' from there they came into Aelron. 'tis said they're lookin' fer an intr'ductin t' th' Blue Wizard. Got some business from th' Emperor."

"A gift, I am told, a bribe, but for what?"

"I dunno."

"Discover this and be rewarded. Fail and face the consequences."

"Aye m'lord!"

As usual, there came the queer feeling at the end of these meetings, like something tickled his brain, at first it was pure pleasure, like nothing he'd ever experienced before; then it became otherworldly, repellant and it made him scream and void the contents of belly, bowel and bladder.

The chair rejected him and he slumped to the floor crawling out into the hallway where he lay for the better part of an hour in a puddle of his own filth before he could gather the strength to stagger outside.

As he passed the snaggle toothed woman, she cackled:

"Did ya again, did he? You love bein' his bottom boy don't ya?" She cackled maniacally, eye blazing red and a thin black serpentine tongue lolling from her mouth.

Stanbury staggered off to a ramshackle bathhouse, paid his

two coppers and stripped off for a rinse and a soak. While there the slaves washed his grimy clothes and hung them by the fire to dry. When he finally emerged, feeling less clean than he looked, he struggled into his damp clothes and left. It wasn't long before he picked up Korvus' trail and spent the better part of the night wrapped in a thin cloak as he shivered in the cold night air. An hour past dawn Korvus and company emerged from the inn, saddled up and rode north east. Stanbury ran to the stable, entered the third stall, knocked twice then twice more on the wall, and was let in.

The room was cramped, small and stunk like a chicken coop, not surprising as it held a dwarf and four cages of pigeons.

"Send word, there's five of them, two women, three men, they're headed north-east."

"Got it." Replied the dwarf who scribbled a note on a scrap of paper, rolled it into a scroll and attached it to a nearby pigeon. They slipped out of the cubby hole and walking outside the stables, the dwarf oriented himself for a moment then threw the pigeon into the air. Within seconds it had flown out of sight.

"They'll receive it within the hour. Hopefully it'll be enough time."

Ω

"It'll be well past mid-day by the time we reach Nasinar, but we shouldn't

have any problems getting a boat." Intef was saying.

Korvus didn't say much, his head hung down and all he had to eat or drink was water.

"Korvus, what's the matter with you? You haven't said more than a

dozen words all day."

"I want to die. I want the thunder god to stop trying to escape from my

brain."

"Hurts that bad does it?"

"Mmm.'

"Think I got something for ya." He leaned back, opening a saddle bag and rooted around. After a minute or two he came up with a glazed clay bottle corked shut.

"Hold out your hand." Korvus did. Intef poured some yellowish powder in it.

"Put that in your mouth and wash it down with water."

"What is it?"

"Powdered essence of willow bark. It'll ease your headache."

Korvus knocked it back and almost coughed it out immediately. But he managed to choke down a few gulps of water before he gasped out;

"That was terrible! It was the most bitter thing I've ever tasted!"

"Yup, but it'll do the trick, just wait a little while."

True to his word, roughly half an hour later Korvus' headache was gone.

They knew he was feeling better when he began to sing. To say it

was bad would be demeaning to all the bad singers in the world. He voice was raucous and harsh, he could neither carry a tune nor find one, but he made up for it with enthusiasm and joy.

When he finally paused for breath the rest of the group begged him to stop.

"It was like being stuck...in a well with a dozen crows." Snickered Intef.

"Angry crows." Koino added.

Nîlo chimed in; "A dozen angry crows with throat problems!"

"You can all go f..." at that moment the brigands swarmed out of the woods. Two stood before them waving bright cloths and shouting which caused the horses, startled by the noise and confusion, to panic.

A pair emerged from either side and a third pair, bearing spears, brought up the rear, barring any escapes.

Sarafina mentally threw an assailant back 100 yards through the woods, Nîlo did the same, only his man went straight up, at the same moment, he slid from his horse and brandished an oversized razor in each hand.

Korvus leapt from his bucking horse before it threw him and clashed with the nearest brigand while Intef fought for control of his horse.

Koino, cool headed as usual, managed to get off two arrows as her horse reared and plunged, one of her arrows stuck in a brigand's leg while the second was lost. Dropping her bow as she flipped off of her horse's back, her ninjato swept from its scabbard and took off her brigand's left arm; he collapsed howling.

Nîlo ducked the sweep of a brigand's two-handed sword, danced in slashing open the man's unprotected belly with one razor then hamstringing him with the second. Korvus dodged his panicked horse, which continued to buck and kick, then dove at his assailant exchanging a flurry of ringing blows until Korvus maneuvered him near the horse who, obligingly kicked him, then with a powerful blow Korvus decapitated the man. A bit winded, he paused to notice Intef standing over a brigand who'd been gutted like a fish. The rest of the brigands fled. At that moment there was a crashing overhead and a screaming body came plummeting down, splattering all over the road behind them.

"Wow," was all Intef could say.

The sun was beating down when the travelers reached the gates of Nasinar. It was an cosmopolitan city as it had been settled by people from the south and east of Gend, from the deserts of Gohavara, the people of the Jal'harad steppes and drifters from the Northern Confederation.

A port city, it sees it's fair share of newcomers and strangers and the five of them passed through the gates unheeded.

Before long they found the main road to the docks and there stabled the horses at a middling inn, ate a bite and sipped cool drinks

under a striped awning while listening to the locals talk.

After a time Intef got up and sauntered off to the docks.

"I have an errand to run." Stated Koino and left.

Korvus took a long sip of his ale and said; "What are you two up to?"

The pair glanced at each other and shrugged.

"I suppose we could go to the marketplace and pick up some supplies." Nîlo ventured.

"Good idea. I think I'm going to stroll around town and size the place up, who knows what I'll find."

"Be careful," warned Sarafina, "Keep your head down, or whatever it is you do. Stay out of trouble."

Korvus put on an innocent face; "Why I'm hurt!"

"Yeah", Nîlo quipped, "it's like she knew you."

With a hrumph, Korvus swallowed the last of his ale and stalked off into the crowd.

"C'mon, let's hit the market place before he does something stupid and we have to bail him out of trouble."

Sarafina laughed; "I was only kidding."

"It'll happen, you'll see."

Ω

Korvus strolled through the marketplace, pausing to buy a few apples. He munched on one as he walked, drinking in the sights and sounds of Nasinar's bazaar. Accents from all over the empire were here, many with a northern drawl. Eventually he sat under the awning of a tavern sipping cider and watching the city stroll by.

It wasn't long before he spotted what he wanted; a wealthy merchant flaunting his (probably) ill-gotten wealth. He knew the type by sight: garish clothes, too much jewelry, servants and sycophants swarming around while he's being carried in an ornate litter idly snacking on dates from a plate held by a scantily clad female slave. He waited until they'd passed by a fair distance then got up and followed. He kept them in eyesight as he pretended to peruse his surroundings (and kept an eye out for possible escape routes) until they stopped before the doors of a townhouse with a walled courtyard. Alongside the doors stood two bored looking mercenaries, obviously not happy with their guard duties. They half-heartedly saluted as the merchant clambered out, tugging on the slave-girl's chain and strutted through his doors, which shut out the sycophants, who clamored in the street.

Korvus strolled on by, not paying them any attention and rounded the corner. As soon as he was out of sight, he scrambled atop the enclosing wall and hopped down into a lush garden; hearing voices he slid beneath a hedge and watched through an opened door.

The merchants passed by it trailed by a slave with a wax tablet and stylus in hand.

"Send word to Ilos that I shall not attend the Grand Agitor's summer solstice dinner party as conflicting business prevents me. Give him my full apologies and send him that nubile bed slave I bought today. She ought to be able to sooth any rough feathers he has." The merchant's voice grew louder as the pair came into the garden.

"Now, a second letter to the Governor."

"Which one master?"

"Nasinar. Inform him that per our discussion two nights ago I have refused the Grand Agitor's request, opening the way for him to gain an admittance (The Grand Agitor's dinners were for a specific number of guests, usually 11 and it distressed him greatly when this could not occur).

"Let him know I am most delighted to support him in his desire to finally meet His Holiness in person, and hope that one day the favor can be returned."

The merchant stood beside a dwarf date palm and chose a few ripe fruits which he ate, spitting the seeds on the ground.

"Water," he said.

The slave with the tablet left, returning a moment later with a flagon and a blue glass cup. The merchant took it and drained it in a few swallows.

It took very little time for Koino to find Nasinar's "Little Yamato." She'd been aware that Munzo Tahashi's men had been following them for a while and had spotted several of them in a crowd when they entered the city.

She stopped in a small noodle shop, ordered some cold noodles with soya and some tea then waited for nightfall. In the darkness it didn't take her long to lose her 'tail' and she became his shadow, following him to the house of her would-be stalkers.

Through slits in the bamboo shades she could see that there were lamps and candles lit.

Though she made no sound, she knew that they were aware of her and were waiting. Silently she eased a few feet nearer the house then froze in place, spotting a lone figure.

He was still as a statue, relieved only by slow shallow breaths, leaning against a tree not 10' from the veranda.

In three feline steps she was on him; hand clamped over his mouth her dagger a single thrust under the jaw and into his brain. She slowly placed him on the ground, pulled out her dagger and moved on.

In perfect silence she ascended the veranda to the thatch roof and peered down, finding tiny openings in the old thatch. She could see a man kneeling, one hand resting on his sword hilt; he slowly turned his head this way and that, as though listening for something. Drawing out her slim blowgun and a small pack of needles, she carefully took aim at the man and quick puff of breath later found

him slumped against the floor.

She instantly leapt down from the roof and scuttled under the house; inside his companion called out a name but received no answer.

The two men left alive inside grew tense.

Koino drew out her metsubishi and soon found a small gap in the floor.

She stuck one end of the blowgun against the gap and the other end in the metsubishi. Moving as far out of the way as she could, she scraped the underside of the floor with a stick near the metsubishi. She did it again, on the third time she was rewarded when a sword blade was shoved down to the ground through the floor. She gave a low moan, as the blade was withdrawn, counted three heartbeats and blew into the metsubishi.

The poisonous powder blew through the blowgun hole and into the face of the swordsman, who choked, gouging at his eyes which burned as though aflame. Blood poured from his eye sockets, nose and ears; in seconds he was dead.

Rolling out from under the house Koino brushed herself off and walked up to the front door which slid aside with a whisper. A large candle burned on an iron stand, the sweep of her ninjato extinguished it, she silently moved on.

There was only one other room with light, she could hear a woman's harsh breaths in the evening's silence. Noting her silhouette against the shoji, she stabbed swiftly, but to no effect, the figure neatly ducked rolled and moved. She threw the door open with a loud clack and leapt at her.

Their swords clashed, sprang back and clashed again.

"Wait."

The woman gave a slight bow, never taking her eyes off of Koino.

"You are Kirinso Koino, said to be one of the best woman ninja of our time. By killing you I gain honor among our people and I prove my worth to my master."

Koino carefully looked her over, her eyes became steel.

"No. You will lose. You are too young and lack experience, you will only die."

"I disagree, I've practiced for many years, I am Hittaro Ren-o and I am ready, even if you are not." rising, she loosened the kusari-gama in her hand and began to whirl the chain. Koino stood her ground, all senses alert, she began to sweat; she was the better swordsman, but she'd never faced an opponent with this chain-and-sickle weapon before and had no idea how to defend against it; Koino feinted, Hittaro swung and scored a cut on Koino's right shoulder, but the favor was returned an instant later with a slash to Hittaro's left thigh; backing away from the onslaught, Koino kicked over a wide candle on it's iron stand and a third of the room became dark. Hittaro increased the power of her attack and Koino found the chain wrapped around her right arm to the shoulder, the sickle a few inches from her throat. Deftly drawing a wakizashi from her belt, Koino scored with a slice along Hittaro's ribs cage which burned but wasn't deep. When the younger woman backed off, Koino freed her arm then maneuvering around, she split a second candle in two with a stroke of her sword. Now only a small pool of light lay in the room. Koino backed away, fading into the darkness.

Hittaro stared wildly about first left then right, the chain whirling, ever moving as she waited. Suddenly Koino was behind her, whispering her name as the cold steel of Hittaro's own kusari-gama slipped effortlessly around her throat.

Her last sight was Koino stepping briefly into the light and she saw no more.

Finding paper, ink and brush she sat at a low desk and began to write:

"Shintaro Aemon, called Munzo Tahashi;

This is the fate of all who oppose me.

Send word to your master to cease his foolish vendetta, it will not stop me and it will not save him."

She blew out the candle.

Ω

Wanting to catch the mariners at first light the group decided to camp on the beach.

From somewhere Intef produced wooden bowls and half a loaf of hard bread. Once the soup was done boiling he ladled it out, broke off a hunk of bread and passed it around. In short time everyone was "mmm-ing" over the soup and talk faded. Korvus had pulled out a dagger and quickly fashioned two pair of crude chopsticks for he and Koino while the others used their bread or their fingers to eat the solid parts of the soup.

"What gives?" Intef more or less said around a mouthful of soupy bread.

"Barbarian," returned Korvus and deftly plucked a morsel of meat from his soup with his chopsticks and popped it into his mouth.

"I've heard that in Ilos they're using small pitchforks to eat with now instead of knives and spoons," Nîlo said.

Intef chuckled and shook his head.

"You know how it is in Ilos, always trying to be 'modern' and 'progressive,' like those ridiculous pantaloons that were popular a few years ago with those *pockets* in them. Pockets, who needs 'em, I ask you?"

The conversation turned to gossip about lord such-and-such who was going to wed lady so-and-so and was the Emperor really going to raise taxes again this year and other inconsequential talk. A skin of wine made an appearance and after being passed around a few time the laughter grew apace.

"Do you remember the time..."

was said, as was "...and that time when you..."

The night went on, the moon was sinking out of sight and Sarafina began to yawn, resting her head on Nîlo's shoulder, soon she was snoring.

Likewise, Korvus yawned, stood up and stretched (a little unsteadily).

"I'll take first watch." Koino said throwing another log on the fire.

Korvus yawned again; "I'll take second."

"I guess I'm third." Muttered Intef as he settled into his bedroll.

Nîlo shook Sarafina and stood up, pulling her to her feet.

She groaned, but stood.

"Sorry girl, but it's bed time for me." He led her to her bedroll then went to his own and was soon asleep.

Sarafina stood before her unmade bedroll and sulked quietly for a few minutes before she'd gotten the curséd thing straitened out and was snoring before she knew it.

Ω

Hittaro Ren-o woke alone. Her throat was chaffed raw where the chain of the kusari-gama constricted it. Dismal, but determined by her failure to kill Kirinso Koino, she gathered herself together and thats when she found the note.

"I swear by the Buddha Amida I will find you and kill you for this. My soul and my honor demand it."

She folded the note carefully and prepared for her return to her master Shintaro, knowing his anger would be great however she was prepared to pay that price just to satisfy her own thirst for vengeance.

Two days later she knelt in the street before the doors of an elaborate inn in Nasinar's Yamatotown. On the veranda two samurai stood stern and immutable; the three of them waited in the hot sun, they standing, her kneeling.

The door slid aside and a samurai emerged, followed by Shintaro Aemon dressed in a light blue kimono accented with phoenixes done in gold thread. After a servant brought out a thick cushion, a second bringing a tray with tea, he sat and gave some brief orders to his two men then deigned to notice her.

"So, she escaped you." He popped open a jet black fan decorated with crimson dragon flies and fanned himself.

"Yes lord." Hittaro said, bowing again. Sweat trickled down her face, she refused to notice it.

He paused, sipping his tea and rereading the note. The fan rustled like an injured raven's wing.

"She must be stopped. I give you one last try. I will send two men with you who are exceptional in their skills. Perhaps you can learn something from them as you hunt her down."

"I will not fail you a second time my lord." Head bowed to ground, resting on her folded hands before her.

"I want her head. It would be better if you could bring her back alive, but I hold no illusions."

"Her head lord, yes."She sat back up. The fan moved laconically.

"Hittaro-san, if you cannot perform this task, kill yourself at once."

"It will be done."

She was absolutely sure that if she failed and did not commit seppuku, the two would do it for her; either way she would be dead if she failed.

Ω

A s their breakfast was settling Intef and Korvus spent several hours of laconic haggling, the old man parted with his rickety boat for 10 gold pieces, a sack of flour and six wrinkled apples. The backpacks and their owners were stowed in the boat and shoved off.

Assured that they would reach the island before nightfall, everyone seemed to be in high spirits.

"I hate this wretched thing!" Nîlo sat with his head sling low, slowly turning green with each gentle wave that rocked the boat.

"The water is so beautiful and you can see clear to the bottom!"

Korvus paused in his rowing to look .

"Wow, look at that turtle, its huge!" The boat began to veer off course as Intef had kept rowing.

"Korvus we're off course!"

"Sorry." He pulled at his oar and the boat straightened out.

A stiff breeze rushed around them, cooling the warmth of the day a bit and making the voyage more pleasant.

"Ooh gods below!" Nîlo spun around and leaned far over the railing, spewing into the pristine waters.

Koino sighed and shook her head.

The mountain in the midst of the waters slowly grew closer, it was lush and green with heavy vegetation and a few sails could be seen off its shores. Roughly halfway there Koino and Nîlo took over the rowing letting the other two rest.

"Do I have to row?"

"Nîlo, it'll take your mind off your stomach, now grab a handful of oar and pull."

There was a shifting of seats and a scary moment with the boat being tipsy, but as soon as everyone sat, it was fine.

Sarafina trailed her hand in the water.

"Korvus, look, she said quietly. They were delighted to see a number of small gold and blue striped fish swim up to investigate her fingers, that is until

"Ow! That one bit me!" She yanked her hand out and sure enough there was a tiny scallop of a wound on her finger. The small fish swarmed around the boat for a time but when no more prospects of a meal appeared, they drifted away.

"Remind me never to go skinny

continued on page 121

TIME
2: NEMESIS
A Novel
By Shawn M. Tomlinson

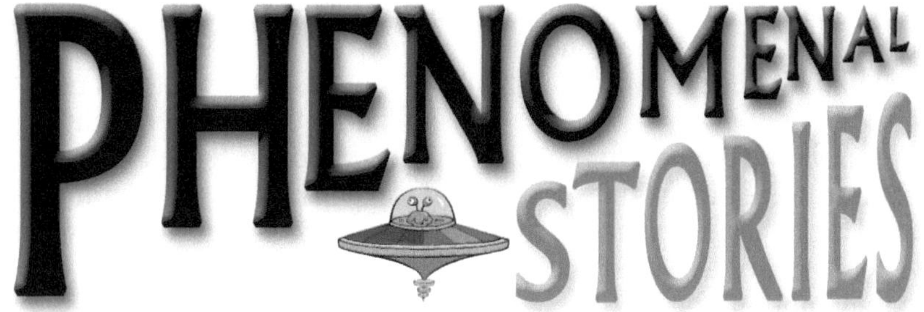

Zirl & Sons Publishers

Time

Book 02: Nemesis

By Shawn M. Tomlinson

(Part 3 of 8)

Chapter 10

"It's not fair that we didn't get to say goodbye to Jebba, Trevor and Alan," Chloe said, sounding as she did on rare occasion, like a pouty child. "And why in hell is that woman riding with us?"

"Calm, calm, my darling," Martin said. "First, we've got to get moving if we are going to be in a position to help or rescue or whatever our friends. Ted wanted to immerse them in the military... ambiance..." he said smiling "without interruption. He thought that the crash course for three such seasoned operatives would be best, so that meant once they were inside the bunker, it was the last we were going to see of them for a while.

"Second, Alex isn't that bad. She pissed me off about back East, but she's smart and trustworthy. You may even come to like her."

"Fat bloody effing chance of that," Chloe said, using her newly discovered "swear" word, kind-of testing it out.

She had discovered that Martin would not say certain words in front of her, but sometimes used them with other people when he thought she couldn't hear him. There was one such word that made her flush open-mouthed. She could hardly believe Martin used it. It came in the middle of his most-often used

phrase, which around Chloe was "Bloody Effing Hell." Although "effing" was unfamiliar to her, once she heard him use the real word, she got it.

When she used it now for the first time in front of him as they walked toward the house, he gave her a sidelong look, smiled that crooked smile and they continued.

"Alex wants you to go with her, not be with me."

Martin laughed, but not much. He needed to sooth Chloe.

"She may want me to go back East, but she certainly doesn't *want* me," Martin said calmly. "And why on earth would you think for even a split second that I would want her?"

"You did," Chloe said angrily. "She's made that very clear."

Martin did laugh loudly this time.

"Did she say when that was, by any chance?" he asked, still laughing, which made Chloe even more angry.

"No," Chloe said.

"We were 5 years old in kindergarten!" Martin said.

"What?" Chloe asked.

"The last time I saw Alex before the Fall, we were 16 and playing in a very bad band together," Martin said. "She certainly didn't have any interest in me then, and probably never did. The last time I had any interest in her was kindergarten. I swear."

Chloe, calmer now, asked, "Then why does she act like you had some torrid effing affair?"

"Probably to see you turn that deep shade of red and purple when she says it," Martin said. "Look, after The Fall, she ran into me — literally — as she was running away from some very bad people.

"After that war — it was near the end battle that we met again — she trained and got herself pretty good at weapons and diplomacy and stuff. She managed to finagle her way into some of the missions I went on, out here. I did trust her, still do. She's good in a fight, but not like you. She's very smart and that helps in many circumstances."

"So, she went into Cheyenne Mountain with you the first time?" Chloe asked.

"She did," Martin said. "She used her charms on the new guy in charge, Gen. Thompson, after Gen. Ramirez took a bullet, and I think she helped solidify the alliance. Alex stayed out here for a while, but she always felt uneasy, so she went back East. We made do without her.

"The thing is, my darling, don't let her get to you. She likes to play games, and you don't, so of course she tries to get to you. Don't let her. I never did."

"Too bad she doesn't get an urgent effing message to go back where she feels safe," Chloe pondered aloud.

"We may need her, so she can leave as soon as we're done," Martin said. "She will, too, because she likes it back there. I think the only reason she's here now is because the Powers That Be thought her previous experience with NORAD might help. And it might. I also know that, while I cannot depend upon her like I do you, she has got my back, yours, too. She won't betray us and she'll stick with it as long as we do."

"I still don't like her," Chloe confirmed.

"Don't need to," he said, smiling at her and embracing her warmly. "We need her, she needs us, then she'll be gone."

"And you don't want to go back East?" Chloe said with fear slightly trembling her voice a little.

"Not a chance," Martin said. "If you, by some chance and strange circumstances, ever want to visit there, I'll go with you... for a very short time. Maybe you'll want to see what civilization actually looks like in this Time. Maybe not. If you do, I will reluctantly take you there, but we're not staying."

He unlocked the door to the house and they went in. They removed their dusters. They always wore them when they went out for shooting practice because, as Martin said, the extra weight and bulk would make them faster when they weren't wearing them.

"Why is this place 'back East' so special?" Chloe asked, sitting down beside him on the sofa.

"OK, so, you've read about Rome, right?" he asked, pulling her small form onto his lap.

"Modern or ancient?"

"Ancient."

"Yes, Roman Empire and all that, but not much," Chloe confirmed.

"OK, Rome ruled a wide area for a long time," Martin began. "The Romans even brought a kind of oppressive peace to a wide region, called *Pax Romana*. A Roman citizen could travel anywhere in the empire safely because if anyone harmed him or her, the full might of the empire would descend upon the entire region where the event occurred.

"Power. Then, Rome began to fall, not all at once, but the empire kept shrinking until Rome itself finally fell. The result was a centuries-long Dark Age. Civilization, at least in Europe, had to start all over, and without virtually any technology, it took a long, long time.

"OK, so speed ahead to the world of the early 21st century. Nobody called themselves an empire, but there were empires just the same. The United States, basically, was the biggest, most powerful one."

"That's where we are, right?" she asked.

"Yep," he said, "it was here. I grew up in the most technologically advanced civilization there ever had been. Like Rome, though, it started to crumble. Not just here, though, everywhere. No one knows why, exactly. So some people saw it coming..."

"Like you," she said.

"Yes, but I wasn't in a position to do anything about it," he said. "I didn't have a lot of money and no power, so I was just waiting for it to happen. I was a lot different, back then.

"Anyway, the folks that did have money and some power, started a sanctuary in the mountains not that far from where I grew up. I ended up inside the boundaries of the new organization. It's a long story, but to shorten it a lot, I managed to become kind of integral to the whole thing. See, I'd envisioned something very similar myself, but just couldn't come up with the resources to do it.

"The idea was to create a safe place with all the best scientists, engineers and other big thinkers inside to work toward shortening by a long way the approaching Dark Age. It seemed like a good idea at the time. It *was* a good idea, but I guess any time someone grabs complete power over the lives of the people, it turns bad.

"When I started to see that happening, I took myself out of the succession to the throne."

"You... you are a prince?" Chloe said, looking at him anew.

He laughed, said, "Not exactly. Just made myself useful when things were at their worst, and pretty soon, everyone was talkin' about me being the heir apparent.

"I suppose that there once was a time, when I was very young, that that would have appealed to me, in theory anyway. By the time it happened, I wanted nothing to do with it.

"As I said, I've changed a lot."

Martin looked deeply and carefully into Chloe's eyes, said, "You wouldn't have given me the time of day if you'd met me before The Fall."

"What does that mean?"

"You wouldn't even have noticed me or cared if you did," he explained. "Wouldn't blame ya."

"I can't believe you were such bad person," Chloe said, kissing him.

"I wasn't bad exactly," Martin said, "probably a much worse person now, actually. No, I just wasn't much to look at or anyone of interest. I probably thought I was, but in retrospect, I wasn't. Just a loser who thought he could take pictures."

"You take very good pictures," she said, "and you could not possibly have been a 'loser.' You are the most amazing man I've ever met."

"Thanks, but that's probably not true," he said. "Ted's a much better leader than I am. Burnside's much more charming."

"Crazy talk," she said, hugging him tightly.

"I think one day, perhaps, we will go 'back East,'" she said. "I'd really like to see this place you walked away from. Not that I want to stay, but I'd like to tell them all just how much they lost."

"Thanks," he said, kissing her again.

"Now what about this trial?" she asked.

"I've killed people," he said. "You know it. You've seen me do it. I don't like it and avoid it as much as possible, but it does happen.

"Someone thought that what I did at Lake Tahoe a few years back was murder. It wasn't. The guy was shooting at everyone and couldn't be talked down. Funny thing is, I didn't kill him. I was out of bullets. Those around me were low, too. I didn't have a Glock back then, so I had very few shots to begin with. I'm not sure who got the guy, but I'm not sorry. He had a mountain of ammunition that we found afterward. If someone hadn't taken him out, he'd have killed us all."

"So, they want you back for a trial for a crime you didn't commit?" Chloe asked incredulous.

"Yep," he said. "Can't prove my innocence, though, so no way to go back.

"Things are different out here in the New Old West, as you've seen repeatedly. I've done lots of things I don't like, but everything I've done, I pretty much had to do.

"I don't drink much, so I never got into bar fights, and I never went looking for a fight. Those back East are all civilized now, and most of them have never been in situations like we have. I guess I don't recognize them as any sort of authority over me anymore."

"You don't need to," she said. "You beat yourself up enough. It's just us, now. Once we get finished with this current business, I want it to be just us. I will marry you and we will have a good life together. I'm certain of that. No more Easterners coming to break up our happy home. Just us."

"It sounds perfect to me," he said, grabbing her into a very tight embrace.

They didn't have long for tender moments. They were leaving at first light, just ahead of Jebba, Trevor and Alan.

Chloe and Martin made dinner together, ate together, then retired early.

They didn't let go of each other all night.

Chapter 11

Alex was knocking on the door of the house just as the first glimmers of dawn were springing up from the east.

Behind her there were several assault vehicles and several Humvees. All told, there were 25 of them — including Chloe, Martin and Alex — going to Colorado.

Breakfast had been quick so that Martin and Chloe could check and arrange their weapons. Aside from those they carried routinely, they packed extra Glocks and a lot of bullets. Martin had packed 12 of the purple-white grenades he'd used in the mountains near Lake Sumner. He showed Chloe basically how to use them, made sure she carried six on her.

Together they carried the case with the extra weapons and bullets out to the Humvee, put it in the back.

"You drive, Martin," Alex said. "You're better at it than me. And I assume Chloe wants the shotgun seat, so I'll ride behind her."

Chloe thought Alex was being a little too accommodating, but didn't argue.

A Major Briggs came to speak with them, snapped Martin a salute.

"Better get out of that habit," Martin told him. "I'm not a general anymore, major."

"Sir," Briggs said. "We'll follow your planned route. I'll be in the lead vehicle with you behind and the others behind you. We do have communications between vehicles, so if we need to change plans we can do it on the fly."

"Thank you, major," Martin said and joined Chloe and Alex in the Humvee.

The plan was vague at best, Martin thought. His group was moving into Colorado and beyond Cheyenne Mountain to the west to liberate prisoners they'd discovered through

Ted Williams says...
Make Mine
MOXIE
MOXIE
Original

scouts. There were hundreds of them, probably rounded up from nearby mostly, but Carrie said a raid had captured some of her people at Salt Lake City.

That wasn't planned, and some of the Easterners — who weren't trained militarily — would break if tortured. That could give at least bits of technology Shaw shouldn't have. Carrie wanted Martin and his group to rescue them before Shaw had them sorted out from the rest and before they could be tortured.

Martin wasn't sure Shaw would bother with torture. He probably would just crucify all of them in some big show, possibly just east of Salt Lake City where they could be discovered easily by his enemies.

Rescuing the prisoners was the main goal, and Major Briggs had several large empty trucks in their convoy to hold them and bring them back to the safety of the bunker.

The other goal, though, was to then turn east to come at NORAD from the north and to be there to act as support for Jebba, Trevor and Burnside and their group if they needed help.

Martin wasn't certain yet how they were going to help them if that group was inside the mountain when things went south. He'd figure it out, he figured, and he was used to winging it. He just hoped Gen. Trevor and crew could make everything work smoothly inside the mountain with Shaw. It was difficult to predict a paranoid effing jerk.

Martin, Chloe, Alex and a squad of soldiers would be coming over the mountains near NORAD when the main body of the convoy returned to the bunker. At least that was Martin's plan, although he hadn't told Briggs about it yet.

Chloe had possession of a small blue rectangular plastic box that she kept secured on her body under her left breast. She wanted to make certain no one could get it unless she was dead.

The box had been rigged by Jebba as a simple beacon. She had a similar, purple box, and Trevor and Burnside each had their own.

Chloe could feel the slight vibration of the energy inside the thing, or, probably, just thought she could. If it vibrated strongly, it was a signal from one of her friends.

"I know we can't exactly talk between us when we're inside the mountain," Jebba told her a few days before, "but I've made up these rudimentary communicators so we have some idea about each other. All I could put inside each was the stuff to have a direct line between us, a panic button and a GPS thing. I didn't put audio in it because any or all of us may be in a position where a sudden alert sound could get us killed."

"What's 'GPS?'" Chloe had asked.

"Global positioning satellite, it stands for," Jebba said. "Apparently, the satellites — up in orbit around the planet — haven't failed yet, which is surprising, so we can know exactly where each of us is. That is, if their orbits haven't shifted too much."

"I'm feeling like a 19th century girlee again," Chloe admitted to Jebba.

Jebba flashed a big smile again, said, "In the late 20th century, many of the countries launched these big computer things into space, into orbit around the planet. Each one of them could do a whole bunch of things. Mostly they were for global communications and TV signals, but a couple or a few of them together could communicate with each other and with GPS devices on the ground. For GPS, the satellites receive signals from your device on the ground wherever you are, then talk to the other buggers and between them they can determine exactly where you are in longitude and latitude.

"So, OK, we're both standing here together in the desert south of Fort Sumner, New Mexico, so the satellites see us as being in the same place. If you're here and I'm at Salt Lake City, the satellites see us in two different places with different coordinates. They then can tell us how far apart we are and, given the right software, provide a map to show us how to get to each other."

"OK, that makes some sense," Chloe said. "I'll have to read about it, I think, then I'll know it."

"Martin has at least one book about it," Jebba said. "I saw it, thought I was going to have to use it, but Ted – when he knew what I needed – took me to the bunker's stores and I got complete GPS circuits. Didn't have to do it from scratch, which I appreciated.

"I used some old portable hard drive enclosures. Can't imagine hard drives being this big and still being called 'portable,' but that's what Martin said they were. The good thing is they're mostly plastic, so I'm hoping that any security sensors Shaw might use won't spot them as a threat.

"So, OK, if it vibrates violently – keep it on your body somewhere – that means we're in trouble and heading out of NORAD the best we can. I built in a small screen on the reverse. It will give a very small map of the area and light up with dots for each of us: purple for me, yellow for Trevor, orange for Alan.

"I've done some fiddling with the primitive circuits, so you should be able to zoom in using this touch bit here. That will bring it down to street level so you can see which way we're going.

"I don't really expect that, if we're running, we'll live, but if we signal you and are moving slowly, it probably will mean that we are making our way out without being harassed by Shaw. If he acts civilized and lets us go normally, I won't send the vibration signal until we reach the five-mile point."

Jebba handed the device to Chloe.

"You're gonna get out of there," Chloe said. "I know it."

"I think so, too," Jebba said, "but I wanted to make sure we had some little contact between us."

"Shouldn't Martin have one of these, too?" Chloe asked.

"I actually didn't think of that," Jebba laughed. "I guess I think of you two as one person these days, since you're always together. Well, you'll have to operate it for both of you. My guess is that when I see your little light on my device, I'm seeing Martin, too."

Chloe hugged Jebba tightly. Jebba no longer even minded, and hugged her back.

"Now don't forget," Jebba said. "Lady Marion has gone to a lot of trouble to give you the biggest, grandest wedding she can, so you and Martin need to be there. Alive. Don't get dead, as he says."

"You need to be there, too," Chloe said, "so you stay upright as well."

Jebba snort-laughed, said, "I'll be seein' ya soon, Chloe," and got in a waiting vehicle to be driven back to the bunker.

Chapter 12

"How far is it to where we're going?" Alex was yelling from the rear seat of the Humvee.

"Total of around 400 miles," Martin said, "probably another 375. Are you bored already?"

"Lonely back here," she said, winking at him in the rear view mirror.

"Take a nap," Chloe suggested.

Despite being in a convoy, they were moving at quite a clip.

The roads weren't that bad, and all the military vehicles were built for rough terrain anyway, so they made good time.

Ted had told them that, under good conditions, they could make Cheyenne Mountain in about six or seven hours, but they weren't going the direct route.

The plan was for them to turn off the main road – Route 25 – at Walsenburg and head west along Route 160. They were to continue through the mountains to Fort Garland, then to Alamosa.

Carrie had shown them maps and photographs. The prisoners were being marched on foot across what had been Interstate 70. That meant they were moving through some of the harshest desert around, then into and over the mountains to reach NORAD.

Martin's group would head north from Alamosa using Route 17, then 285, then Route 24 to, hopefully, arrive in Avon, Colorado, before the Salt Lake Death March reached the place.

Since most of the prisoners were on foot – herded by Shaw's soldiers in vehicles – they knew it would take many days to traverse the more than 600-mile distance.

As it was, Martin's group would have taken two days to get to Avon.

Chloe still marveled at the countryside and always felt pangs of sadness when they passed through towns that had fallen to ruins.

There still were people in Alamosa, and some at Salida and Buena Vista, but most areas were devoid of human inhabitants.

They stayed just outside Alamosa to the north where nobody was around the first night. The soldiers unpacked the popup living quarters for them and then busied themselves with their own camp. Chloe was pleased to see that Alex had a separate popup from her and Martin. She'd dreaded spending a night with the woman.

continued on page 112

PHENOMENAL STORIES

ZIRL & SONS PUBLISHERS

God Editor of Doom's Note: For various reasons, a lot of great stories have entered the Public Domain. That means anyone can use them without permission or payment to the estate of the author. I should feel guilty about using such stories, but so many pieces of my writing have ended up being stolen and printed without my permission or payment to me that I no longer do. So, we have the opportunity to present some great early works by some fantastic authors in Phenomenal Stories. E. Hoffman Price was a member of the Lovecraft Circle, a good friend of H.P. Lovecraft's and the only member of the Circle to meet in person the Weird Tales Big Three: Lovecraft, Clark Ashton Smith and Robert E. Howard. He recounted his membership in the Circle along with his views of the three writers in his wonderful book, The Book of the Dead. While many writers wrote stories in view of HPL, few collaborated with him directly. This is one such case.

Through the Gates of the Silver Key

By H.P. Lovecraft & E. Hoffman Price

Original Publication: Weird Tales, July 1934

(Conclusion)

Chapter Five

A sudden shutting-off of the waves left Carter in a chilling and awesome silence full of the spirit of desolation. On every hand pressed the illimitable vastness of the void; yet the seeker knew that the Being was still there. After a moment he thought of words whose mental substance he flung into the abyss: "I accept. I will not retreat."

The waves surged forth again, and Carter knew that the Being had heard. And now there poured from that limitless Mind a flood of knowledge and explanation

which opened new vistas to the seeker, and prepared him for such a grasp of the cosmos as he had never hoped to possess. He was told how childish and limited is the notion of a tri-dimensional world, and what an infinity of directions there are besides the known directions of up-down, forward-backward, right-left. He was shown the smallness and tinsel emptiness of the little Earth gods, with their petty, human interests and connections - their hatreds, rages, loves and vanities; their craving for praise and sacrifice, and their demands for faiths contrary to reason and nature.

While most of the impressions translated themselves to Carter as words there were others to which other senses gave interpretation. Perhaps with eyes and perhaps with imagination he perceived that he was in a region of dimensions beyond those conceivable to the eye and brain of man. He saw now, in the brooding shadows of that which had been first a vortex of power and then an illimitable void, a sweep of creation that dizzied his senses. From some inconceivable vantagepoint he looked upon prodigious forms whose multiple extensions transcended any conception of being, size and boundaries which his mind had hitherto been able to hold, despite a lifetime of cryptical study. He began to understand dimly why there could exist at the same time the little boy Randolph Carter in the Arkham farm-house in 1883, the misty form on the vaguely hexagonal pillar beyond the First Gate, the fragment now facing the Presence in the limitless abyss, and all the other Carters his fancy or perception envisaged.

Then the waves increased in strength and sought to improve his understanding, reconciling him to the multiform entity of which his present fragment was an infinitesimal part. They told him that every figure of space is but the result of the intersection by a plane of some corresponding figure of one more dimension - as a square is cut from a cube, or a circle from a sphere. The cube and sphere, of three dimensions, are thus cut from corresponding forms of four dimensions, which men know only through guesses and dreams; and these in turn are cut from forms of five dimensions, and so on up to the dizzy and reachless heights of archetypal infinity. The world of men and of the gods of men is merely an infinitesimal phase of an infinitesimal thing - the three-dimensional phase of that small wholeness reached by the First Gate, where 'Umr at-Tawil dictates dreams to the Ancient Ones. Though men hail it as reality, and band thoughts of its many-dimensioned original as unreality, it is in truth the very opposite. That which we call substance and reality is shadow and illusion, and that which we call shadow and illusion is substance and reality.

Time, the waves went on, is motionless, and without beginning or end. That it has motion

and is the cause of change is an illusion. Indeed, it is itself really an illusion, for except to the narrow sight of beings in limited dimensions there are no such things as past, present and future. Men think of time only because of what they call change, yet that too is illusion. All that was, and is, and is to be, exists simultaneously.

These revelations came with a god like solemnity which left Carter unable to doubt. Even though they lay almost beyond his comprehension, he felt that they must be true in the light of that final cosmic reality which belies all local perspectives and narrow partial views; and he was familiar enough with profound speculations to be free from the bondage of local and partial conceptions. Had his whole quest not been based upon a faith in the unreality of the local and partial?

After an impressive pause the waves continued, saying that what the denizens of few-dimensioned zones call change is merely a function of their consciousness, which views the external world from various cosmic angles. As the Shapes produced by the cutting of a cone seem to vary with the angles of cutting - being circle, ellipse, parabola or hyperbola according to that angle, yet without any change in the cone itself - so do the local aspects of an unchanged - and endless reality seem to change with the cosmic angle of regarding. To this variety of angles Of consciousness the feeble beings of the inner worlds are slaves, since with rare exceptions they can not learn to control them. Only a few students of forbidden things have gained inklings of this control, and have thereby conquered time and change. But the entities outside the Gates command all angles, and view the myriad parts of the cosmos in terms of fragmentary change-involving perspective, or of the changeless totality beyond perspective, in accordance with their will.

As the waves paused again, Carter began to comprehend, vaguely and terrifiedly, the ultimate background of that riddle of lost individuality which had at first so horrified him. His intuition pieced together the fragments of revelation, and brought him closer and closer to a grasp of the secret. He understood that much of the frightful revelation would have come upon him - splitting up his ego amongst myriads of earthly counterparts inside the First Gate, had not the magic of 'Umr at-Tawil kept it from him in order that he might use the silver key with precision for the Ultimate Gate's opening. Anxious for clearer knowledge, he sent out waves of thought, asking more of the exact relationship between his various facets - the fragment now beyond the Ultimate Gate, the fragment still on the quasi-hexagonal pedestal beyond the First Gate, the boy of 1883, the man of 1928, the various ancestral beings who had formed his heritage and the bulwark of his ego, amid the nameless denizens of the other eons and other worlds which that first hideous flash ultimate perception had identified with him. Slowly the waves of the Being surged out in reply, trying to make plain what was almost beyond the reach of an earthly mind.

All descended lines of beings of the finite dimensions, continued the waves, and all stages of growth in each one of these beings, are merely manifestations of one archetypal and eternal being in the space outside dimensions. Each local being - son, father, grandfather, and so on - and each stage of individual being - infant, child, boy, man - is merely one of the infinite phases of that same archetypal and eternal being, caused by a variation in the angle of the consciousness-plane which cuts it. Randolph Carter at all ages; Randolph Carter and all his ancestors, both human and pre-human, terrestrial and pre-terrestrial; all these were only phases of one ultimate, eternal "Carter" outside space and time - phantom projections differentiated only by the angle at which the plane of consciousness happened to cut the eternal archetype in each case.

A slight change of angle could turn the student of today into the child of yesterday; could turn Randolph Carter into that wizard, Edmund Carter who fled from Salem to the hills behind Arkham in 1692, or that Pickman Carter who in the year 2169 would use strange means in repelling the Mongol hordes from Australia; could turn a human Carter into one of those earlier entities which had dwelt in primal Hyperborea and worshipped black, plastic Tsathoggua after flying down from Kythamil, the double planet that once revolved around Arcturus; could turn a terrestrial Carter to a remotely ancestral and doubtfully shaped dweller on Kythamil itself, or a still remoter creature of trans-galactic Stronti, or a four-dimensioned gaseous consciousness in an older space-time continuum, or a vegetable brain of the future on a dark, radioactive comet of inconceivable orbit - so on, in endless cosmic cycle.

The archetype, throbbed the waves, are the people of the Ultimate Abyss - formless, ineffable, and guessed at only by rare dreamers on the low-dimensioned worlds. Chief among such was this informing Being itself... which indeed was Carter's own archetype. The gutless zeal of Carter and all his forebears for forbidden cosmic secrets was a natural result of derivation from the Supreme Archetype. On every world all great wizards, all grcat thinkers, all great artists, are facets of It.

Almost stunned with awe, and with a kind of terrifying delight, Randolph Carter's consciousness did homage to that transcendent Entity from which it was derived. As the waves paused again he pondered in the mighty

silence, thinking of strange tributes, stranger questions, and still stranger requests. Curious concepts flowed conflictingly through a brain dazed with unaccustomed vistas and unforeseen disclosures. It occurred to him that, if these disclosures were literally true, he might bodily visit all those infinitely distant ages and parts of the universe which he had hitherto known only in dreams, could he but command the magic to change the angle of his consciousness-plane. And did not the silver key supply that magic? Had it not first changed him from a man in 1928 to a boy in 1883, and then to something quite outside time? Oddly, despite his present apparent absence of body; he knew that the key was still with him.

While the silence still lasted, Randolph Carter radiated forth the thoughts and questions which assailed him. He knew that in this ultimate abyss he was equidistant from every facet of his archetype - human or non-human, terrestrial or extra-terrestrial, galactic or trans-galactic; and his curiosity regarding the other phases of his being - especially those phases which were farthest from an earthly 1928 in time and space, or which had most persistently haunted his dreams throughout life - was at fever heat. He felt that his archetypal Entity could at will send him bodily to any of these phases of bygone and distant life by changing his consciousness-plane and despite the marvels he had undergone he burned for the further marvel of walking in the flesh through those grotesque and incredible scenes which visions of the night had fragmentarily brought him.

Without definite intention he was asking the Presence for access to a dim, fantastic world whose five multi-coloured suns, alien constellations, dizzily black crags, clawed, tapir-snouted denizens, bizarre metal towers, unexplained tunnels, and cryptical floating cylinders had intruded again and again upon his slumbers. That world, he felt vaguely, was in all the conceivable cosmos the one most freely in touch with others; and he longed to explore the vistas whose beginnings he had glimpsed, and to embark through space to those still remoter worlds with which the clawed, snouted denizens trafficked. There was no time for fear. As at all crises of his strange life, sheer cosmic curiosity triumphed over everything else.

When the waves resumed their awesome pulsing, Carter knew that his terrible request was granted. The Being was telling him of the nighted gulfs through which he would have to pass of the unknown quintuple star in an unsuspected galaxy around which the alien world revolved, and of the burrowing inner horrors against which the clawed, snouted race of that world perpetually fought. It told him, too, of how the angle of his personal consciousness-plane, and the angle of his consciousness-plane regarding the space-time elements of the sought-for world, would have to be tilted simultaneously in order to restore to that world the Carter-facet which had dwelt there.

The Presence wanted him to be sure of his symbols if he wished ever to return from the remote and alien world he had chosen, and he radiated back an impatient affirmation; confident that the silver key, which he felt was with him and which he knew had tilted both world and personal planes in throwing him back to 1883, contained those symbols which were meant. And now the Being, grasping his impatience signified its readiness to accomplish the monstrous precipitation. The waves abruptly ceased, and there supervened a momentary stillness tense with nameless and dreadful expectancy.

Then, without warning, came a whirring and drumming that swelled to a terrific thundering. Once again Carter felt himself the focal point of an intense concentration of energy which smote and hammered and seared unbearably in the now-familiar rhythm of outer space, and which he could not classify as either the blasting heat of a blazing star, or the all-petrifying cold of the ultimate abyss. Bands and rays of colour utterly foreign to any spectrum of our universe played and wove and interlaced before him, and he was conscious of a frightful velocity of motion. He caught one fleeting glimpse of a figure sitting alone upon a cloudy throne more hexagonal than otherwise...

Chapter Six

As the Hindoo paused in his story he saw that de Marigny and Phillips were watching him absorbedly. Aspinwall pretended to ignore the narrative and kept his eyes ostentatiously on the papers before him. The alien-rhythmed ticking of the coffin-shaped clock took on a new and portentous meaning, while the fumes from the choked, neglected tripods wove themselves into fantastic and inexplicable shapes, and formed disturbing combinations with the grotesque figures of the draft-swayed tapestries. The old Negro who had tended them was gone - perhaps some growing tension had frightened him out of the house. An almost apologetic hesitancy hampered the speaker as he resumed in his oddly labored yet idiomatic voice.

"You have found these things of the abyss hard to believe," he said, "but you will find the tangible and material things ahead still barer. That is the way of our minds. Marvels are doubly incredible when brought into three dimensions from the vague regions of possible dream. I shall not try to tell you much - that would be another and very different story. I will tell only what you absolutely have to know."

Carter, after that final vortex of alien and polychromatic rhythm,

had found himself in what for a moment he thought was his old insistent dream. He was, as many a night before, walking amidst throngs of clawed, snouted beings through the streets of a labyrinth of inexplicably fashioned metal under a plate of diverse solar colour; and as he looked down he saw that his body was like those of the others - rugose, partly squamous, and curiously articulated in a fashion mainly insect-like yet not without a caricaturish resemblance to the human outline. The silver key was still in his grasp, though held by a noxious-looking claw.

In another moment the dream-sense vanished, and he felt rather as one just awakened from a dream. The ultimate abyss - the Being - the entity of absurd, outlandish race called Randolph Carter on a world of the future not yet born - some of these things were parts of the persistent recurrent dreams of the wizard Zkauba on the planet Yaddith. They were too persistent - they interfered with his duties in weaving spells to keep the frightful Dholes in their burrows, and became mixed up with his recollections of the myriad real worlds he had visited in light-beam envelopes. And now they had become quasi-real as never before. This heavy, material silver key in his right upper claw, exact image of one he had dreamt about meant no good. He must rest and reflect, and consult the tablets of Nhing for advice on what to do. Climbing a metal wall in a lane off the main concourse, he entered his apartment and approached the rack of tablets.

Seven day-fractions later Zkauba squatted on his prism in awe and half despair, for the truth had opened up a new and conflicting set of memories. Nevermore could he know the peace of being one entity. For all time and space he was two: Zkauba the wizard of Yaddith, disgusted with the thought of the repellent earth-mammal Carter that he was to be and had been, and Randolph Carter, of Boston on the Earth, shivering with fright at the clawed, snouted thing which he had once been, and had become again.

The time units spent on Yaddith, croaked the Swami - whose laboured voice was beginning to show signs of fatigue - made a tale in themselves which could not be related in brief compass. There were trips to Stronti and Mthura and Kath, and other worlds in the twenty-eight galaxies accessible to the light-beam envelopes of the creatures of Yaddith, and trips back and forth through eons of time with the aid of the silver key and various other symbols known to Yaddith's wizards. There were hideous struggles with the bleached viscous Dholes in the primal tunnels that honeycombed the planet. There were awed sessions in libraries amongst the massed lore of ten thousand worlds living and dead. There were tense conferences with other minds of Yaddith, including that of the Arch-Ancient Buo. Zkauba told no one of what had befallen his personality, but when the Randolph Carter facet was uppermost he would study furiously every possible means of returning to the Earth and to human form, and would desperately practice human speech with the alien throat-organs so ill adapted to it.

The Carter-facet had soon learned with horror that the silver key was unable to effect his return to human form. It was, as he deduced too late from things he remembered, things he dreamed, and things he inferred from the lore of Yaddith, a product of Hyperborea on Earth; with power over the personal consciousness-angles of human beings alone. It could, however, change the planetary angle and send the user at will through time in an unchanged body. There had been an added spell which gave it limitless powers it otherwise lacked; but this, too, was a human discovery - peculiar to a spatially unreachable region, and not to be duplicated by the wizards of Yaddith. It had been written on the undecipherable parchment in the hideously carven box with the silver key, and Carter bitterly lamented that he had left it behind. The now inaccessible Being of the abyss had warned him to be sure of his symbols, and had doubtless thought he lacked nothing.

As time wore on he strove harder and harder to utilize the monstrous lore of Yaddith in finding a way back to the abyss and the omnipotent Entity. With his new knowledge be could have done much toward reading the cryptic parchment; but that power, under present conditions, was merely ironic. There were times, however, when the Zkauba-facet was uppermost and when he strove to erase the conflicting Carter-memories which troubled him.

Thus long spaces of time wore on - ages longer than the brain of man could grasp, since the beings of Yaddith die only after prolonged cycles. After many hundreds of revolutions the Carter-facet seemed to gain on the Zkauba-facet, and would spend vast periods calculating the distance of Yaddith in space and time from the human Earth that was to be. The figures were staggering eons of light-years beyond counting but the immemorial lore of Yaddith fitted Carter to grasp such things. He cultivated the power of dreaming himself momentarily earthward, and learned many things about our planet that he had never known before. But he could not dream the needed formula on the missing parchment.

Then at last he conceived a wild plan of escape from Yaddith - which began when be found a drug that would keep his Zkauba-facet always dormant, yet with out dissolution of the knowledge and memories of Zkauba. He thought that his calculations

H.P. Lovecraft

E. Hoffman Price

would let him perform a voyage with a light-wave envelope such as no being of Yaddidi had ever performed - a bodily voyage through nameless eons and across incredible galactic reaches to the solar system and the Earth itself.

Once on Earth, though in the body of a clawed, snouted thing, he might be able somehow to find and finish deciphering-the strangely hieroglyphed parchment he had left in the car at Arkham; and with its aid - and the key's - resume his normal terrestrial semblance.

He was not blind to the perils of the attempt. He knew that when he had brought the planet-angle to the right eon (a thing impossible to do while hurtling through space), Yaddith would be a dead world dominated by triumphant Dholes, and that his escape in the light-wave envelope would be a matter of grave doubt. Likewise was he aware of how he must achieve suspended animation, in the manner of an adept, to endure the eon long flight through fathomless abysses. He knew, too, that - assuming his voyage succeeded - he must immunize himself to the bacterial and other earthly conditions hostile to a body from Yaddith. Furthermore, he must provide a way of feigning human shape on Earth until he might recover and deci-

pher the parchment and resume that shape in truth. Otherwise he would probably be discovered and destroyed by the people in horror as a thing that should not be. And there must be some gold - luckily obtainable on Yaddid - to tide him over that period of quest

Slowly Carter's plans went forward. He prepared a light-wave envelope of abnormal toughness, able to stand both the prodigious time-transition and the unexampled flight through space. He tested all his calculations, and sent forth his Earthward dreams again and again, bringing them as close as possible to 1928. He practiced suspended animation with marvelous success. He discovered just the bacterial agent he needed, and worked out the varying gravity-stress to which he must become used. He artfully fashioned a waxen mask and loose costume enabling him to pass among men as a human being of a sort, and devised a doubly potent spell with which to hold back the Dholes at the moment of his starting from the dead, black Yaddith of the inconceivable future. He took care, too, to assemble a large supply of the drugs - unobtainable on Earth - which would keep his Zkauba-facet in abeyance till he might shed the Yaddith body, nor did he neglect a small store of gold for earthly use.

The starting-day was a time of doubt and apprehension. Carter climbed up to his envelope-platform, on the pretext of sailing for the triple star Nython, and crawled into the sheath of shining metal. He had just room to perform the ritual of the silver key, and as he did so he slowly started the levitation of his envelope. There was an appalling seething and darkening of the day, and hideous racking of pain. The cosmos seemed to reel irresponsibly, and the other constellations danced in a black sky.

All at once Carter felt a new equilibrium. The cold of interstellar gulfs gnawed at the outside of his envelope, and he could see that he floated free in space - the metal building from which he had started having decayed years before. Below him the ground was festering with gigantic Dholes; and even as he looked, one reared up several hundred feet and leveled a bleached, viscous end at him. But his spells were effective, and in another moment he was falling away from Yaddith, unharmed.

Chapter Seven

In that bizarre room in New Orleans, from which the old black servant had instinctively fled, the odd voice of Swami Chandraputta grew hoarser still.

"Gentlemen," he continued, "I will not ask you to believe these things until I have shown you special proof. Accept it, then, as a myth, when I tell you of the thousands of light-years - thousands

continued on page 141

PHENOMENAL STORIES

ZIRL & SONS PUBLISHERS

God Editor of Doom's Note: Our intrepid travel columnist, who likes to go by the name Intrepid, after some harrowing bouts with pseudo-reality, found himself back home a few centuries from now, but even there, he couldn't get a "normal" vibe from his surroundings. Even the GEOD couldn't help, as if he ever did. A new "ally" made things all the creepier. Here's part one of Intrepid's latest dispatch...

My New Bestest Buddy

By J.D. Hayes-Canell

I smelled a rat.

There had to be more to it than Atticus "Ben" Bradley just wanting to, ahem, learn from me.

We'd never really gotten a long that well, but we'd never been enemies exactly, either. There was plenty of that in the newsroom. Legendary assassinations by paper cut, ugly lethal presses in the presses, sending someone off to die the agonizingly slow and horrifying "death by board meeting..." There were a million ways to die in the cutthroat publishing world. Always had to watch one's back.

Atticus hadn't chosen any of those lethal things, though, at least not yet. Maybe he thought cozying up to me would get him in Mathandy's dress, either personally or sexually?

Again, the strong stench of a well-manicured, Armani-wearing greasy rat hit me across the car from Atticus "Ben" Bradley.

Whatever the game, needed to be on my toes, and other clichés,

but needed gallons of coffee to do that. As soon as a couple dozen supersized cupfuls had passed my lips, I'd be ready.

I tried to settle in as he repeated the direction request for the computer and off we went soundlessly. The scenery slid by, empty, meaningless. Glaring neon, dystopian holographic billboards advertising things in a dozen different languages, people wandering the streets, and the bum again.

Something just didn't "feel" right...

"What would you like?" Atticus asked me, a gentle touch on the back of my hand.

Startled out of my mental meanderings I noticed we'd stopped at a café.

"I... I... coffee, light, two sugars, large."

I eased my hand away, trying to be casual about it. He smiled indulgently, repeated my order. "And I will have a cappuccino sotto voce con leche."

Seconds later the order arrived in warm thermo cups.

"Yours is bigger," Atticus mentioned with a small smile handing me my cup.

"Yes. I like it that way," I replied, suddenly aware of a subtle undercurrent to our conversation, and not-quite comfortable with it... at all.

"Sharon, resume ride."

"Of course sir."

Without a sound or barely a quiver, we sped on. It was dreamlike watching the city pass, so easy to ignore. Atticus was speaking again:

"...find it helps to sooth my nerves. Do you believe so? I know so little about you."

"I'm sorry, I was thinking about this story, I missed what you were saying."

"Classical music," he said a touch exasperated, "I find it to be relaxing."

"Some of it yes," I said. "I like some Debussy when I'm writing at home, unless I'm working on my novel, then it's Wagner all the way."

"Really, I would've taken you for a Brahms or Beethoven fan."

"You have arrived at your final destination," Sharon stated in her too melodious voice.

"Excellent, not a moment too soon," Atticus remarked as the door whispered open and the belts released with a serpentine hiss.

I scrambled out of the car, gasping and clutching my coffee. Not my day, it tasted burnt and bitter. Past caring, I drank it anyway. Now that I thought about it, did I ever finish the Cat article? I'm sure I did.

I connected with my personal data base and scanned. Nope, nowhere. There's an outline with numerous corrections and rewrites, but not a trace of the article itself, yet I knew I wrote it and submitted it.

"I'll worry about it later," I said aloud.

"What's that?"

"Oh, I was talking to myself. I

PS#01 Sep 2018 · Vol. 1, No. 1
Cover: Cara Nilsen

PS#02 Oct 2018 · Vol. 1, No. 2
Cover: Cara Nilsen

PS#03 Nov 2018 · Vol. 1, No. 3
Cover: Shawn M. Tomlinson

PS#04 Dec 2018 · Vol. 1, No. 4
Cover: Savn C. Crishnan

PSQ#01 Win 2018 · Vol. 1, No. 1
Cover: Gary W. Ziroli

LC#01 Win 2018 · Vol. 1
Cover: Shawn M. Tomlinson

PS#05 Jan 2019 · Vol. 2, No. 1
Cover: Savn C. Crishnan

PS#06 Feb 2019 · Vol. 2, No. 2
Cover: Savn C. Crishnan

PS#07 Mar 2019 · Vol. 2, No. 3
Cover: Savn C. Crishnan

PSQ#02 Spr 2018 · Vol. 2, No. 1
Cover: Shawn M. Tomlinson

PS#08 Apr 2019 · Vol. 2, No. 4
Cover: Savn C. Crishnan

PS#09 May 2019 · Vol. 2, No. 5
Cover: Savn C. Crishnan

PS#10 Jun 2019 · Vol. 2, No. 6
Cover: Savn C. Crishnan

PSQ#03 Sum 2019 · Vol. 2, No. 2
Cover: Gary W. Ziroli

PS#11 Jul 2019 · Vol. 2, No. 7
Cover: Carole A. Tomlinson

PNM#01 Jul 2019 · Vol. 1, No. 1
Cover: Cara Nilsen

PS#12 Aug 2019 · Vol. 2, No. 6
Cover: Gary W. Ziroli

PFM#1 Aug 2019 · Vol. 1, No. 1
Cover: Shawn M. Tomlinson

PS#13 Sep 2019 · Vol. 2, No. 9
Cover: Savn C. Crishnan

PNM#02 Sep 2019 · Vol. 1, No. 2
Cover: Savn C. Crishnan

The Phenomenal Magazine Group

Zirl & Sons Publishers
A Subsidiary of
Zirlinson Publishing

wrote an article about Mrs. Hackenpuss and her cats, but I can't locate it."

"Odd that."

"Yup. Odd."

We walked up the 27 (yes I counted them) steps to the front door of the mansion. A pair of rookie cops were standing guard. I flashed my credentials, they smirked.

Atticus flashed his and suddenly they were ushering us in. One was murmuring into his comm, so the others knew we were coming.

Two men in white uniforms were towing a hover-gurney, atop which was a large economy-sized body bag. It was chilling to think Mrs Hackenpuss was in there. The gurney men were followed by a quintet of cats, meowing loudly and eyeing the gurney hungrily.

Behind them came the coroner and the detective. The coroner nodded to us and kept on going. The detective stopped and glared.

"What do you want? What are you doing here?"

"My, you are full of questions aren't you, I assume that's why you're a detective," my companion said.

I stared at Atticus.

"Not the way I would've gone about that, but you do you," I said quietly to him.

"Let's get this out of the way," the detective said. "One, I hate reporters. Two, this is a highly sensitive matter and so you are doubly not welcome. Three, I personally do not want you here. So, there are three good reasons for you to leave. Now."

"Well, freedom of the press is still a thing, so I don't think we will," I said.

Atticus tried to brush past him, but the detective shot out a hand and grabbed him by the arm. I gasped. Atticus' suit cost more than most people make in five years, and it just got wrinkled.

Atticus looked like he'd stepped barefoot in dog poop and wrenched his arm free.

Then several things happened: Atticus slipped a hand into his jacket pocket, the detective yanked a gun out of his holster while simultaneously shoulder blocking me and I collapsed on the ground as he drew on Atticus. Atticus ever so slowly drew out his confabulator and showed it to the detective, then he made a call, the detective never wavered, at least not until his phone rang. He touched his ear to answer it.

"Yeah (pause) but it's a fresh crime scene (pause) yeah, yes... yes. Alright, bu..."

His mouth closed up like a little draw purse. He holstered his weapon.

"I don't know who you spoke to or how you influenced them, but you have 10 minutes to look over the crime scene and then leave or I will have you sent to the front!"

"Of the house?" I asked totally confused.

"No, you idiot, the front lines. You report the news, but don't read the news or watch TV? Are you aware that we were recently

attacked by the Free Rattus Liberation Front?"

"Who?"

"We had a treaty with the government of Rattusmagna, didn't care that the guy was a tyrant we backed him because he claimed to be running a democracy. The people revolted, there was a coup, the Ratts (That's what they call themselves) took over and tried to boot us out."

"Ah yes, I recall reading that in the New NewJersey Herald," Atticus said. "Our scientists had discovered huge deposits of Caseusum and we had permits to mine. Their miners' union was quite happy with it if memory serves."

Atticus looked pleased with himself.

"Isn't caseusum essential to our lunar colonies?" I asked.

"Yes, it is, they can't do a thing without it." He smiled a bit at me and said:

"Time's wasting, let's go look at our murder scene."

"Not a homicide!"

"That's what you say now."

"Ten minutes!" he snarled.

We walked through the place, footsteps echoing in the empty rooms. We'd taken a wrong turn and wound up in the service area where the servants cooked and laundered and did whatever the servants of the wealthy do.

"Weird."

"What is?" Atticus asked.

"For someone who had so many cats you wouldn't think she'd have a problem with mice." I pointed out several large mousetraps along the floor.

"Not mice, rats."

"Eew."

We entered the kitchen. The chef was standing before the stove stirring a large pot. His toque was the puffy cloth kind. On him it looked like a deflated albino soufflé. It almost covered his head like a hood.

"Cooking something for the staff?" I asked.

"Yes," the chef replied peering down into his pot. "It was originally for Madam Hackenpuss, but that's not going to happen. So as not to waste good food I shall serve it to the staff."

"Smells good, what is it?"

"Ratatouilles."

"Of course it is," I said and I heard a rim shot in my head.

We moved along out to the pool. There was a row of three chaise lounges with awnings.

"You can tell which one was hers," I said pointing at one as big as a queen-sized bed.

The table next to her lounge was covered with medicine bottles, a half liter bottle of Diet Fresca™ and a small vat of sun screen.

"Why me?" I said to Atticus.

"Excuse me?"

"There are a half-dozen better reporters you could've done this with, why did you chose me?"

"I told you, Mathandy is saying her farewells and you need a partner."

"I don't need a partner, haven't

had a partner in the seven years I've worked here. What are you after?"

"You're familiar with the 'Law of the Jungle.'"

"Eat or be eaten."

"More or less, or you could say that 'Only the strong survive'."

"Are you after my job? You have more influence with the GEOD than I could ever hope for, why do you need my job?"

"You're an achiever Trep, you're climbing the ladder, you're going the Blue Collar route, whereas I took the White Collar route and received what is my due. Only that doesn't seem to appease him."

His head fell forward and he heaved a sigh.

He didn't have to tell me who 'he' was.

"I must appear to look productive or else I will soon find myself out on the street. That will never do, so, I need you to teach me how to do your job."

"Why would I do something like that?"

"If you don't, not only will the GEOD get a first-hand look at your expenses in Mordor, but I'm sure that Angela will be terribly upset to discover that she's been fired for sexual harassment by you."

"Say what now?" Atticus continued to scan the ground

"I already have witnesses who will gladly testify to the H.R. person with written documentation and pictures that show her acting inappropriately in the workplace.

"Since the most damning evidence comes from you, complete with your signature and DNA scan, it's a sure thing she'll be thrown out into the street, where she will lose her apartment, her chihuahua, her car, her self esteem, because no one will believe her protests of innocence, she will become unhireable."

My mouth dropped open. I couldn't fathom this kind of thing happening to me. I was stunned. As though we'd been talking about the weather, he pointed and said: "There," he husked pointing at the ground. I looked and saw nothing at first.

"Look close."

I bent down, faint scrape marks on the ferrocrete.

"Four of them," I said.

"No, two sets, like a pair of toenails dragging."

"If they were dragging her that means she'd have to have been unconscious or already dead and whoever did it dragged her to the pool to make it look like a drowning!"

I was snapping holo's like crazy.

There was a clatter behind us and a shriek followed by screams of pain. We ran. Inside the ratatouilles had boiled over on to the floor and was smelling burnt, the kitchen was filling up with smoke. The shrieks of pain continued, we followed them and the detective burst in just as we had.

Before our eyes, lying on the floor was the chef with both feet and one hand caught in rat traps.

His oversized floppy toque fell off and we could see his long pointed nose, beady eyes, whispy mustache and oversized ears.

The detective gasped, “A Rattusmagnanian!”

Near him lay a small bottle. The Detective picked it up.

“Is this what you fed to Mrs Hackenpuss?”

“No, I don’t know what you’re talking about!”

Atticus and I turned our backs as the detective did something unpleasant with a rat trap.

After screaming so loudly that I had to cover my ears, the chef shrieked: “I confess, I confess, I poisoned her! I had too, it was all the damned cats!”

“Stop, please stop, it was Gerarde, Gerarde, I swear, just stop!”

“Who’s Gerarde?” The cop asked.

“Mrs. Hackenpuss’ nephew, and only surviving relative,” I chimed in.

Cops cuffed the Rattusmaganian and hauled him away.

“We need to get out of here and find her nephew,” I said as quietly as I could.

“You’re going to warn him?”

“No, set up an interview. This is a pretty good lede. I can link it to my previous story about the cats, tie in the war aspect. Do you see how this fits together?”

Atticus gave me a perplexed look, shrugged, said, “I’m sure you will explain it all to me later.”

Turns out Gerarde wasn’t home and no amount of scouring that we did turned him up, never did find out what happened to him.

The ride home was a silent one. Not finding Gerarde, and then getting out of there before the cops caught us (missed us by seconds; we hid behind a dumpster while they broke down the door and began ransacking the place).

As we drove away I spotted the sallow-faced bum again. His face, it’s hard to describe, it’s like he’s wearing a mask, like something inhuman clothed in a human skin. I shivered and turned away before our eyes could meet again.

We got back to EPICAC and I started Atticus out with the basics. Got about a quarter of the way through the article and he yawned.

“I think I’ve had enough excitement for the night,” he said, stretched, yawned again.

Couldn’t help it, I sympathetically yawned.

“Let me know how it turns out, and,” he paused at the door. “Don’t forget to put my name on there.”

He smiled as he left.

There had to be a way out of this. I picked up my confabulator and called Angela.

I woke up early the next morning, called Angela, made last minute plans and we both sped off to work. We were absurdly early, there was only the overnight skeleton crew on, and almost no one in our office. As per my previous night’s request Robo-Sally texted me the minute Atticus walked in the door. I sent her a text back telling him I needed to see him immediately, it was about the article.

Sure as sunrise he rushed into the office, bypassing the bathroom. As he did, out of nowhere Angela was in his arms screaming to beat the band. She pulled him into the bathroom while appearing to struggle against him and screaming "NO!" at the top of her lungs.

I was already stationed in the bathroom with the holocamera and took hundreds of pics of the struggle. The mood was broken when a janitrob came in to clean and recorded what it saw. At that point I popped my head over a stall door, snapped his picture one last time and said: "Surprise. I can send these down to HR at the touch of a button. We wouldn't want that to happen, now would we?"

It was Atticus' turn to be shocked. Outraged, he shoved Angela away and in one motion swiped the holocamera out of my hand and into a toilet where it foamed and burst into flame.

"Doesn't matter," I shrugged with a smile. "They were automatically backed up to my computer as I took them. Methinks the lesson endeth here."

"Yeah, Atticus, take a hike!" Angela tried to sneer. It wasn't pretty.

"Alright Trep, it's a standoff. I'll concede for now, but I'm not going anywhere."

"Fine, don't, but you don't have to be such a jerk. There're nicer ways to have done that."

He paused for a moment and thought.

"Yes, but none as satisfying."

He spun on his heel and strode out.

ZIRL & SONS PUBLISHERS

God Editor of Doom's Note: For various reasons, a lot of great stories have entered the Public Domain. That means anyone can use them without permission or payment to the estate of the author. I should feel guilty about using such stories, but so many pieces of my writing have ended up being stolen and printed without my permission or payment to me that I no longer do. So, we have the opportunity to present some great early works by some fantastic authors in Phenomenal Stories. Here we have another story from ***The King in Yellow*** *that largely has been forgotten. It is a haunting tale in line with if subtler than the other stories from the legendary book.*

Street of the Four Winds

By Robert W. Chambers

"Ferme tes yeux à demi,
Croise tes bras sur ton sein,
Et de ton coeur endormi
Chasse à jamais tout dessein.
"Je chante la nature,
Les étoiles du soir, les larmes du matin,
Les couchers de soleil à l'horizon lointain,
Le ciel qui parle au coeur d'existence future!"

I

The animal paused on the threshold, interrogative, alert, ready for flight if necessary. Severn laid down his palette, and held out a hand of welcome. The cat remained motionless, her yellow eyes fastened upon Severn.

"Puss," he said, in his low, pleasant voice, "come in."

The tip of her thin tail twitched uncertainly.

"Come in," he said again.

Apparently she found his voice reassuring, for she slowly settled upon all fours, her eyes still fastened upon him, her tail tucked under her gaunt flanks.

He rose from his easel smiling. She eyed him quietly, and when he walked toward her she watched him bend above her without a wince; her eyes followed his hand until it touched her head. Then she uttered a ragged mew.

It had long been Severn's custom to converse with animals, probably because he lived so much alone; and now he said, "What's the matter, puss?"

Her timid eyes sought his.

"I understand," he said gently, "you shall have it all at once."

Then moving quietly about he busied himself with the duties of a host, rinsed a saucer, filled it with the rest of the milk from the bottle on the window-sill, and kneeling down, crumbled a roll into the hollow of his hand.

The creature rose and crept toward the saucer.

With the handle of a palette knife he stirred the crumbs and milk together and stepped back as she thrust her nose into the mess. He watched her in silence. From time to time the saucer klinked upon the tiled floor as she reached for a morsel on the rim; and at last the bread was all gone, and her purple tongue travelled over every unlicked spot until the saucer shone like polished marble. Then she sat up, and coolly turning her back to him, began her ablutions.

"Keep it up," said Severn much in-

terested, "you need it."

She flattened one ear but neither turned nor interrupted her toilet. As the grime was slowly removed Severn observed that nature had intended her for a white cat. Her fur had disappeared in patches, from disease or the chances of war, her tail was bony and her spine sharp. But what charms she had were becoming apparent under vigorous licking, and he waited until she had finished before reopening the conversation. When at last she closed her eyes and folded her forepaws under her breast, he began again very gently: "Puss, tell me your troubles."

At the sound of his voice she broke into a harsh rumbling which recognized as an attempt to purr. He bent over to rub her cheek and she mewed again, an amiable inquiring little mew, to which he replied, "Certainly, you are greatly improved, and when you recover your plumage you will be a gorgeous bird." Much flattered she stood up and marched around and around his legs, pushing her head between them and making pleased remarks, to which he responded with grave politeness.

"Now what sent you here," he said, "here into the Street of the Four Winds, and up five flights to the very door where you would be welcome? What was it that prevented your meditated flight when I turned from my canvas to encounter your yellow eyes? Are you a Latin Quarter cat as I am a Latin Quarter man? And why do you wear a rose-colored flowered garter buckled about your neck?" The cat had climbed into his lap and now sat purring as he passed his hand over her thin coat.

"Excuse me," he continued in lazy soothing tones, harmonizing with her purring, "if I seem indelicate, but I cannot help musing on this rose-colored garter, flowered so quaintly and fastened with a silver clasp. For the clasp is silver; I can see the mint mark on the edge, as is prescribed by the law of the French Republic. Now, why is this garter woven of rose silk and delicately embroidered, -- why is this silken garter with its silver clasp about your famished throat? Am I indiscrete when I inquire if its owner is your owner? Is she some aged dame living in memory of youthful vanities, fond, doting on you, decorating you with her intimate personal attire? The circumference of the garter would suggest this, for your neck is thin, and the garter fits you. But then again I notice -- I notice most things -- that the garter is capable of being much enlarged. These small silver-rimmed eyelets, of which I count five, are proof of that. And now I observe that the fifth eyelet is worn out, as though the tongue of the clasp were accustomed to lie there. That seems to argue a well-rounded form."

The cat curled her toes in contentment. The street was very still outside.

He murmured on: "Why should your mistress decorate you with an article most necessary to her at all times? Anyway, at most times. How did she come to slip this bit of silk and silver about your neck? Was it the caprice of a moment, -- when you, before you had lost your pristine plumpness, marched singing into her bedroom to bid her good-morning? Of course, and she sat up among the pillows, her coiled hair tumbling to her shoulders, as you sprang upon the bed purring: 'Good-day, my lady.' Oh, it is very easy to understand," he yawned, resting his head on the back of the chair. The cat still purred, tightening and relaxing her padded claws over his knee.

"Shall I tell you about her, cat? She is very beautiful -- your mistress," he murmured drowsily, "and her hair is heavy as burnished gold. I could paint her, -- not on canvas -- for I should need shades and tones and hues and dyes more splendid than the iris of a splendid rainbow. I could only paint her with closed eyes, for in dreams alone can such colors as I need be found. For her eyes, I must have azure from skies untroubled by a cloud -- the skies of dreamland. For her lips, roses from the palaces of slumberland, and for her brow, snow-drifts from mountains which tower in fantastic pinnacles to the moons; -- oh, much higher than our moon here, -- the crystal moons of dreamland. She is -- very -- beautiful, your mistress."

The words died on his lips and his eyelids drooped.

The cat too was asleep, her cheek turned up upon her wasted flank, her paws relaxed and limp.

II

"It is fortunate," said Severn, sitting up and stretching, "that we have tided over the dinner hour, for I have nothing to offer you for supper but what may be purchased with one silver franc."

The cat on his knee rose, arched her back, yawned, and looked up at him.

"What shall it be? A roast chicken with salad? No? Possibly you prefer beef? Of course, -- and I shall try an egg and some white bread. Now for the wines. Milk for you? Good. I shall take a little water, fresh from the wood," with a motion toward the bucket in the sink.

He put on his hat and left the room. The cat followed to the door, and after he had closed it behind him, she settled down, smelling at the cracks, and cocking one ear at every creak from the crazy old building.

The door below opened and shut. The cat looked serious, for a moment doubtful, and her ears flattened in nervous expectation. Presently, she rose with a jerk of her tail and started on a noiseless tour of the studio. She sneezed at a pot of turpentine, hastily retreating to the table, which she presently mounted, and having satisfied her curiosity concerning a roll of red modelling wax, returned to the door and sat down with her eyes on the crack over the threshold. Then she lifted her voice in a thin plaint.

When Severn returned he looked grave, but the cat, joyous and demonstrative, marched around him, rubbing her gaunt body against his legs, driving her head enthusiastically into his hand, and purring until her voice mounted to a squeal.

He placed a bit of meat, wrapped in brown paper, upon the table, and with a penknife cut it into shreds. The milk he took from a bottle that had served for medicine, and poured it into the saucer on the hearth.

The cat crouched before it, purring and lapping at the same time.

He cooked his egg and ate it with a slice of bread, watching her busy with the shredded meat, and when he had finished, and had filled and emptied a cup of water from the bucket in the sink he sat down, taking her into his lap, where she at once curled up and began her toilet. He began to speak again, touching her caressingly at times by way of emphasis.

"Cat, I have found out where your mistress lives. It is not very far away; -- it is here, under this same leaky roof, but in the north wing which I had supposed was uninhabited. My janitor tells me this. By chance, he is almost sober this evening. The butcher on the rue de Seine, where I bought your meat, knows you, and old Cabane the baker identified you with needless sarcasm. They tell me hard tales of your mistress which I shall not believe. They say she is idle and vain and pleasure-loving; they say she is hare-brained and reckless. The little sculptor on the ground floor, who was buying rolls from old Cabane, spoke to me to-night for the first time, although we have always bowed to each other. He said she was very good and very beautiful. He has only seen her once, and does not know her name. I thanked him; -- I don't know why I thanked him so warmly. Cabane said, 'Into this cursed Street of the Four Winds, the four winds blow all things evil.' The sculptor looked confused, but when he went out with his rolls, he said to me, 'I am sure, Monsieur, that she is as good as she is beautiful.'"

The cat had finished her toilet and now, springing softly to the floor, went to the door and sniffed. He knelt beside her, and unclasping the garter held it for a moment in his hands. After a while he said: "There is a name engraved upon the silver clasp be-

neath the buckle. It is a pretty name. Sylvia Elven. Sylvia is a woman's name, Elven is the name of a town. In Paris, in this quarter, above all, in this Street of the Four Winds, names are worn and put away as the fashions change with the seasons. I know the little town of Elven, for there I met Fate face to face and Fate was unkind. But do you know that in Elven Fate had another name, and that name was Sylvia?"

He replaced the garter and stood up looking down at the cat crouched before the closed door.

"The name of Elven has a charm for me. It tells me of meadows and clear rivers. The name Sylvia troubles me like perfume from dead flowers."

The cat mewed.

"Yes, yes," he said soothingly, "I will take you back. Your Sylvia is not my Sylvia; the world is wide and Elven is not unknown. Yet in the darkness and filth of poorer Paris, in the sad shadows of this ancient house, these names are very pleasant to me."

He lifted her in his arms and strode through the silent corridors to the stairs. Down five flights and into the moonlit court, past the little sculptor's den, and then again in at the gate of the north wing and up the worm-eaten stairs he passed, until he came to a closed door. When he had stood knocking for a long time, something moved behind the door; it opened and he went in. The room was dark. As he crossed the threshold, the cat sprang from his arms into the shadows. He listened but heard nothing. The silence was oppressive and he struck a match. At his elbow stood a table and on the table a candle in a gilded candlestick. This he lighted, then looked around. The chamber was vast, the hangings heavy with embroidery. Over the fireplace towered a carved mantel, gray with the ashes of dead fires. In a recess by the deep-set windows stood a bed, from which the bed-clothes, soft and fine as lace, trailed to the polished floor. He lifted the candle above his head. A handkerchief lay at his feet. It was faintly perfumed. He turned toward the windows. In front of them was a canapé and over it were flung, pell-mell, a gown of silk, a heap of lace-like garments, white and delicate as spiders' meshes, long, crumpled gloves, and, on the floor, beneath the stockings, the little pointed shoes, and one garter of rosy silk, quaintly flowered and fitted with a silver clasp. Wondering, he stepped forward and drew the heavy curtains from the bed. For a moment the candle flared in his hand; then his eyes met two other eyes, wide open, smiling, and the candle flame flashed over hair heavy as gold.

She was pale, but not as white as he; her eyes were untroubled as a child's; but he stared, trembling from head to foot while the candle flickered in his hand.

At last he whispered: "Sylvia, it is I."

Again he said, "It is I."

Then, knowing that she was dead, he kissed her on the mouth. And through the long watches of the night, the cat purred on his knee, tightening and relaxing her padded claws, until the sky paled above the Street of the Four Winds.

PHENOMENAL STORIES

ZIRL & SONS PUBLISHERS

God Editor of Doom's Note: We know that many readers also are writers and some of you may just be starting out. Everybody needs a boost here and there, so our Publisher and Assistant Editor of Pollyannaism, Richard H. Nilsen is here to help. This column is for writers, particularly those beginners who need a little assistance. A lot of the tips and advice, though, work for experienced writers as well.

Reviving the Writers Block

By Richard H. Nilsen

Groups & Workshops & Poets & Writers Oh My: Stuff about writers' groups, workshops and Poets & Writers.

It's especially appropriate that I write about writing workshops for the October issue of **Phenomenal Stories** because I will be overseeing a writing workshop throughout the month of October for Johnstown Public Library (that's Johnstown, NY, not Pennsylvania.)

My writing workshop is modeled on one I started in the 1990s called Writers Block, with the somewhat obvious double meaning of both a blockage in one's writing as well as a group of writers trying to move forward with their writing and publishing.

The original Writers Block was funded through New York State Council on the Arts (NYSCA), while this one is funded through Poets & Writ-

ers Inc.

According to Wikipedia: Poets & Writers Inc. is one of the largest nonprofit literary organizations in the United States serving poets, fiction writers and creative nonfiction writers.

The organization publishes a bi-monthly magazine called Poets & Writers Magazine, and is headquartered in New York City.

It's appropriate that Poets & Writers be involved in this project because I aim to cover most of the writing genres in the workshop.

The only one I have no experience in is screenplay writing.

The "block" part of writing is also appropriate because any group of writers getting together can both foster more writing as well as stilt some writers into a blockage if too much criticism is fostered.

That's one reason my stipulation of "positive" criticism is an important part of the mix.

I have published poetry, novels, memoirs, newspaper features, book reviews, short stories, hundreds of website articles, forewords and introductions to books I've edited and I've even ghost written a couple of books for doctors; one that went on to be a best seller in the CBA:[1] subtitled "The Association for Christian Retail Since 1950." is a trade association that was established in 1950[2].

I actually owned and ran a CBA associated bookstore from 1977 to 1983 and wrote articles and book reviews for their flagship publication, Bookstore Journal.

All the above is meant to show how various writing and publishing can be.

And of course, in the digital age, things have gotten more varied (and actual, physical book reading and book stores have gone through some tough times.)

I would highly encourage anyone interested in writing to attend a local writing group.

There are plenty around you if you just ask at your local library—they may even sponsor one as mine does.

The trick is to balance your creative spirit with what others tell you should be "correct."

You may have to look in on a few different workshops before you find one with the right fit for you.

Meanwhile, plunk your butt in a chair and write.

As the old saying (attributed to a number of writers, including Ernest Hemingway) goes, "Writing is easy... just open a vein."

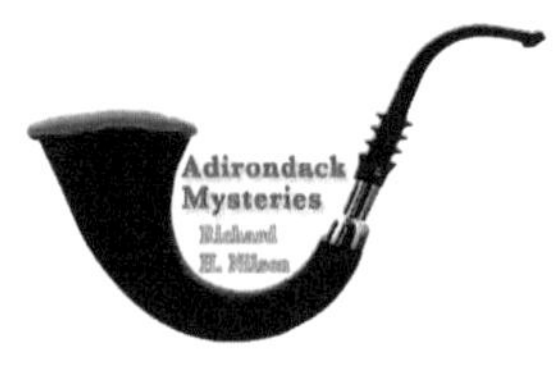

Richard H. Nilsen's works, bio and contact information may be found at richard-h-nilsen.com.

1 CBA (formerly known as the Christian Booksellers Association

2 The association was first organized by 219 Christian bookstores and, by 2011, had grown to include 1700 stores.

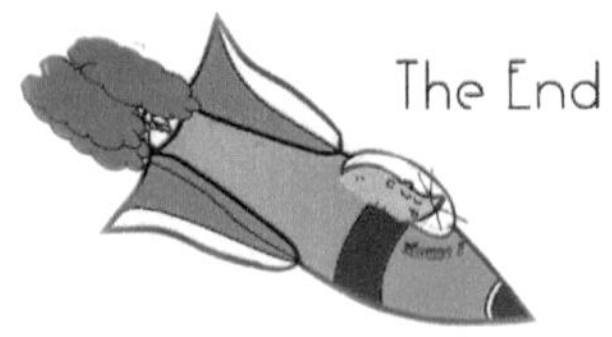

ZIRL & SONS PUBLISHERS

COMING
FOR
YOU!

PHENOMENAL STORIES

ZIRL & SONS PUBLISHERS

God Editor of Doom's Note: For various reasons, a lot of great stories have entered the Public Domain. That means anyone can use them without permission or payment to the estate of the author. I should feel guilty about using such stories, but so many pieces of my writing have ended up being stolen and printed without my permission or payment to me that I no longer do. So, we have the opportunity to present some great early works by some fantastic authors in PHENOMENAL STORIES. *Conan is not my favorite type of fiction, but it is a great example of Robert E. Howard's fiction. Hard edged, intense and intelligent, even if Conan isn't. It is amazing that this only novel Howard ever wrote about Conan is in the Public Domain, but it is. How could we not print it in* PHENOMENAL STORIES?

Hour of The Dragon

By Robert E. Howard

Original Publication: Weird Tales, December 1935 to April 1936; Part 3

Chapter 6

THE THRUST OF A KNIFE

Conan Stooped and tore the knife from the monster's breast. Then he went swiftly up the stair. What other shapes of fear the darkness held he could not guess, but he had no desire to encounter any more. This touch-and-go sort of battling was too strenuous even for the giant Cimmerian. The moonlight was fading from the floor, the darkness closing in, and

'Admit it! Admit it! ABBA still sucks! Admit it!' screamed Conan the Realist to his pal, Dancing Queen

something like panic pursued him up the stair. He breathed a gusty sigh of relief when he reached the head, and felt the third key turn in the lock. He opened the door slightly, and craned his neck to peer through, half expecting an attack from some human or bestial enemy.

He looked into a bare stone corridor, dimly lighted, and a slender, supple figure stood before the door.

"Your Majesty!" It was a low, vibrant cry, half in relief and half in fear. The girl sprang to his side, then hesitated as if abashed.

"You bleed," she said. "You have been hurt!"

He brushed aside the implication with an impatient hand.

"Scratches that wouldn't hurt a baby. Your skewer came in handy, though. But for it Tarascus's monkey would be cracking my shinbones for the marrow right now. But what now?"

"Follow me," she whispered. "I will lead you outside the city wall. I have a horse concealed there."

She turned to lead the way down the corridor, but he laid a heavy hand on her naked shoulder.

"Walk beside me," he instructed her softly, passing his massive arm about her lithe waist. "You've played me fair so far, and I'm inclined to believe in you; but I've lived this long only because I've trusted no one too far, man or woman. So! Now if you play me false you won't live to enjoy the jest."

She did not flinch at sight of the reddened poniard or the contact of his hard muscles about her supple body.

"Cut me down without mercy if I play you false," she answered. "The very feel of your arm about me, even in menace, is as the fulfillment of a dream."

The vaulted corridor ended at a door, which she opened. Outside lay another black man, a giant in turban and silk loincloth, with a curved sword lying on the flags near his band. He did not move.

"I drugged his wine," she whispered, swerving to avoid the recumbent figure. "He is the last, and outer, guard of the pits. None ever escaped from them before, and none has ever wished to seek them; so only these black men guard them. Only these of all the servants knew it was King Conan that Xaltotun brought a prisoner in his chariot. I was watching, sleepless, from an upper casement that opened into the court, while the other girls slept; for I knew that a battle was being fought, or had been fought, in the west, and I feared for you. . . .

"I saw the blacks carry you up the stair, and I recognized you in the torchlight. I slipped into this wing of the palace tonight, in time to see them carry you to the pits. I had not dared come here before nightfall. You must have lain in drugged senselessness all day in Xaltotun's chamber.

"Oh, let us be wary! Strange things are afoot in the palace tonight. The slaves said that Xaltotun slept as he often sleeps, drugged by the lotus of Stygia, but Tarascus is in the palace. He entered secretly, through the postern, wrapped in his cloak which was dusty as with long travel, and attended only by his squire, the lean silent Arideus. I cannot understand, but I am afraid."

They came out at the foot of a narrow, winding stair, and mounting it, passed through a narrow panel which she slid aside. When they had passed through, she slipped it back in place, and it became merely a portion of the ornate wall. They were in a more spacious corridor, carpeted and tapestried, over which hanging lamps shed a golden glow.

Conan listened intently, but he heard no sound throughout the palace. He did not know in what part of the palace he was, or in which direction lay the chamber of Xaltotun. The girl was trembling as she drew him along the corridor, to halt presently beside an alcove masked with satin tapestry. Drawing this aside, she motioned for him to step into the niche, and whispered: "Wait here! Beyond that door at the end of the corridor we are likely to meet slaves or eunuchs at any time of the day or night. I will go and see if the way is clear, before we essay it." Instantly his hair-trigger suspicions were aroused. "Are you leading me into a trap?"

Tears sprang into her dark eyes. She sank to her knees and seized his muscular hand. "Oh, my king, do not mistrust me now!" Her voice shook with desperate urgency. "If you doubt and hesitate, we are lost! Why should I bring you up out of the pits to betray you now?"

"All right," he muttered. "I'll trust you; though, by Crom, the habits of a lifetime are not easily put aside. Yet I wouldn't harm you now, if you brought all the swordsmen in Nemedia upon me. But for you Tarascus's cursed ape would have come upon me in chains and unarmed. Do as you wish, girl."

Kissing his hands, she sprang lithely up and ran down the corridor, to vanish through a heavy double door.

He glanced after her, wondering if he was a fool to trust her; then he shrugged his mighty shoulders and pulled the satin hangings together, masking his refuge. It was not strange that a passionate young beauty should be risking her life to aid him; such things had happened often enough in his life. Many women had looked on him with favor, in the days of his wanderings, and in the time of his kingship.

Yet he did not remain motionless in the alcove, waiting for her return. Following his instincts, he explored the niche for another exit, and presently found one-the opening of a narrow passage, masked by the tapestries, that ran to an ornately carved door, barely visible in the dim light that filtered in from the outer corridor. And as he stared into it, somewhere beyond that carven door he heard the sound of another door opening and shutting, and then a low mumble of voices. The familiar sound of one of those voices caused a sinister expression to cross his dark face. Without hesitation he glided down the passage, and crouched like a stalking panther beside the door. It was not locked, and manipulating it delicately, he pushed it open a crack, with a reckless disregard for possible consequences that only he could have explained or defended.

It was masked on the other side by tapestries, but through a thin slit in the velvet he looked into a chamber lit by a candle on an ebony table. There were two men in that chamber. One was a scarred, sinister-looking ruffian in leather breeks and ragged cloak; the other was Tarascus, king of Nemedia.

Tarascus seemed ill at ease. He was slightly pale, and he kept starting and glancing about him, as if expecting and fearing to hear some sound or footstep.

"Go swiftly and at once," he was saying. "He is deep in drugged slumber, but I know not when he may awaken."

"Strange to hear words of fear issuing from the lips of Tarascus," rumbled the other in a harsh, deep voice.

The king frowned.

"I fear no common man, as you well know. But when I saw the cliffs fall at Valkia I knew that this devil we had resurrected was no charlatan. I fear his powers, because I do not know the full extent of them. But I know that somehow they are connected with this accursed thing which I have stolen from him. It brought him back

to life; so it must be the source of his sorcery.

"He had it hidden well; but following my secret order a slave spied on him and saw him place it in a golden chest, and saw where he hid the chest. Even so, I would not have dared steal it had Xaltotun himself not been sunk in lotus slumber.

"I believe it is the secret of his power. With it Orastes brought him back to life. With it he will make us all slaves, if we are not wary. So take it and cast it into the sea as I have bidden you. And be sure you are so far from land that neither tide nor storm can wash it up on the beach. You have been paid."

"So I have," grunted the ruffian. "And I owe more than gold to you, king; I owe you a debt of gratitude. Even thieves can be grateful."

"Whatever debt you may feel you owe me," answered Tarascus, "will be paid when you have hurled this thing into the sea."

"I'll ride for Zingara and take ship from Kordava," promised the other. "I dare not show my head in Argos, because of the matter of a murder or so -- "

"I care not, so it is done. Here it is; a horse awaits you in the court. Go, and go swiftly!"

Something passed between them, something that flamed like living fire. Conan had only a brief glimpse of it; and then the ruffian pulled a slouch hat over his eyes, drew his cloak about his shoulder, and hurried from the chamber. And as the door closed behind him, Conan moved with the devastating fury of unchained bloodlust. He had held himself in check as long as he could. The sight of his enemy so near him set his wild blood seething and swept away all caution and restraint.

Tarascus was turning toward an inner door when Conan tore aside the hangings and leaped like a blood-mad panther into the room. Tarascus wheeled, but even before he could recognize his attacker, Conan's poniard ripped into him.

But the blow was not mortal, as Conan knew the instant he struck. His foot had caught in a fold of the curtains and tripped him as he leaped. The point fleshed itself in Tarascus's shoulder and plowed down along his ribs, and the king of Nemedia screamed.

The impact of the blow and Conan's lunging body hurled him back against the table and it toppled and the candle went out. They were both carried to the floor by the violence of Conan's rush, and the foot of the tapestry hampered them both in its folds. Conan was stabbing blindly in the dark, Tarascus screaming in a frenzy of panicky terror. As if fear lent him superhuman energy, Tarascus tore free and blundered away in the darkness, shrieking:

"Help! Guards! Arideus! Orastes! Orastes!"

Conan rose, kicking himself free of the tangling tapestries and the broken table, cursing with the bitterness of his blood-thirsty disappointment. He was confused, and ignorant of the plan of the palace. The yells of Tarascus were still resounding in the distance, and a wild outcry was bursting forth in answer. The Nemedian had escaped him in the darkness, and Conan did not know which way he had gone. The Cimmerian's rash stroke for vengeance had failed, and there remained only the task of saving his own hide if he could.

Swearing luridly, Conan ran back down the passage and into the alcove, glaring out into the lighted corridor, just as Zenobia came running up it, her dark eyes dilated with terror.

"Oh, what has happened?" she cried. "The palace is roused! I swear I have not betrayed you -- "

"No, it was I who stirred up the hornet's nest," he grunted. "I tried to pay off a score. What's the shortest way out of this?"

She caught his wrist and ran fleetly down the corridor. But before they reached the heavy door at the other end, muffled shouts arose from behind it and the portals began to shake under an assault from the other side. Zenobia wrung her hands and whimpered.

"We are cut off! I locked that door as I returned through it. But they will burst it in in a moment. The way to the postern gate lies through it."

Conan wheeled. Up the corridor, though still out of sight, he heard a rising clamor that told him his foes were behind as well as before him-

"Quick! Into this door!" the girl cried desperately, running across the corridor and throwing open the door of a chamber.

Conan followed her through, and then threw the gold catch behind them. They stood in an ornately furnished chamber, empty but for themselves, and she drew him to a gold-barred window, through which he saw trees and shrubbery.

"You are strong," she panted. "If you can tear these bars away, you may yet escape. The garden is full of guards, but the shrubs are thick, and you may avoid them. The southern wall is also the outer wall of the city. Once over that, you have a chance to get away. A horse is hidden for you in a thicket beside the road that runs westward, a few hundred paces to the south of the fountain of Thrallos. You know where it is?"

"Aye! But what of you? I had meant to take you with me,"

A flood of joy lighted her beautiful face.

"Then my cup of happiness is brimming! But I will not hamper your escape. Burdened with me you would fail. Nay, do not fear for me. They will never suspect that I aided you willingly. Go! What you have just said will glorify my life throughout the long years."

He caught her up in his iron arms, crushed her slim, vibrant figure to him and kissed her fiercely on eyes, cheeks, throat and lips, until she lay panting in his embrace; gusty and tempestuous as a storm-wind, even his love-making was violent.

"I'll go," he muttered. "But

by Crom, I'll come for you some day!"

Wheeling, he gripped the gold bars and tore them from their sockets with one tremendous wrench; threw a leg over the sill and went down swiftly, clinging to the ornaments on the wall. He hit the ground running and melted like a shadow into the maze of towering rosebushes and spreading trees. The one look he cast back over his shoulder showed him Zenobia leaning over the window-sill, her arms stretched after him in mute farewell and renunciation.

Guards were running through the garden, all converging toward the palace, where the clamor momentarily grew louder-tall men in burnished cuirasses and crested helmets of polished bronze. The starlight struck glints from their gleaming armor, among the trees, betraying their every movement; but the sound of their coming ran far before them. To Conan, wilderness-bred, their rush through the shrubbery was like the blundering stampede of cattle. Some of them passed within a few feet of where he lay flat in a thick cluster of bushes, and never guessed his presence. With the palace as their goal, they were oblivious to all else about them. When they had gone shouting on, he rose and fled through the garden with no more noise than a panther would have made.

So quickly he came to the southern wall, and mounted the steps that led to the parapet. The wall was made to keep people out, not in. No sentry patrolling the battlements was in sight. Crouching by an embrasure he glanced back at the great palace rearing above the cypresses behind him. Lights blazed from every window, and he could see figures flitting back and forth across them like puppets on invisible strings. He grinned hardly, shook his fist in a gesture of farewell and menace, and let himself over the outer rim of the parapet.

A low tree, a few yards below the parapet, received Conan's weight, as he dropped noiselessly into the branches. An instant later he was racing through the shadows with the swinging hill-man's stride that eats up long miles.

Gardens and pleasure villas surrounded the walls of Belverus. Drowsy slaves, sleeping by their watchman's pikes, did not see the swift and furtive figure that scaled walls, crossed alleys made by the arching branches of trees, and threaded a noiseless way through orchards and vineyards. Watch-dogs woke and lifted their deep-booming clamor at a gliding shadow, half scented, half sensed, and then it was gone.

In a chamber of the palace Tarascus writhed and cursed on a blood-spattered couch, under the deft, quick fingers of Orastes. The palace was thronged with wide-eyed, trembling servitors, but the chamber where the king lay was empty save for himself and the renegade priest.

"Are you sure he still sleeps?"

Tarascus demanded again, setting his teeth against the bite of the herb juices with which Orastes was bandaging the long, ragged gash in his shoulder and ribs. "Ishtar, Mitra and Set! That bums like molten pitch of hell!"

"Which you would be experiencing even now, but for your good fortune," remarked Orastes. "Whoever wielded that knife struck to kill. Yes, I have told you that Xaltotun still sleeps. Why are you so urgent upon that point? What has he to do with this?"

"You know nothing of what has passed in the palace tonight?" Tarascus searched the priest's countenance with burning intensity.

"Nothing. As you know, I have been employed in translating manuscripts for Xaltotun, for some months now, transcribing esoteric volumes written in the younger languages into script he can read. He was well versed in all the tongues and scripts of his day, but he has not yet learned all the newer languages, and to save time he has me translate these works for him, to leam if any new knowledge has been discovered since his time. I did not know that he had returned last night until he sent for me and told me of the battle. Then I returned to my studies, nor did I know that you had returned until the clamor in the palace brought me out of my cell." "Then you do not know that Xaltotun brought the king of Aquilonia a captive to this palace?" Orastes shook his head, without particular surprize. "Xaltotun merely said that Conan would oppose us no more. I supposed that he had fallen, but did not ask the details."

"Xaltotun saved his life when I would have slain him," snarled Tarascus. "I saw his purpose instantly. He would hold Conan captive to use as a club against us-against Amalric, against Valerius, and against myself. So long as Conan lives he is a threat, a unifying factor for Aquilonia, that might be used to compel us into courses we would not otherwise follow. I mistrust this undead Pythonian. Of late I have begun to fear him.

"I followed him, some hours after he had departed eastward. I wished to leam what he intended doing with Conan. I found that he had imprisoned him in the pits. I intended to see that the barbarian died, in spite of Xaltotun. And I accomplished -- " A cautious knock sounded at the door. "That's Arideus," grunted Tarascus. "Let him in." The saturnine squire entered, his eyes blazing with suppressed excitement. "How, Arideus?" exclaimed Tarascus. "Have you found the man who attacked me?"

"You did not see him, my lord?" asked Arideus, as one who would assure himself of a fact he already knows to exist. "You did not recognize him?"

"No. It happened so quick, and the candle was out-all I could think of was that it was some devil loosed on me by Xaltotun's magic

-- "

"The Pythonian sleeps in his barred and bolted room. But I have been in the pits." Arideus twitched his lean shoulders excitedly.

"Well, speak, man!" exclaimed Tarascus impatiently. "What did you find there?"

"An empty dungeon," whispered the squire. "The corpse of the great ape!"

"What?" Tarascus started upright, and blood gushed from his opened wound.

"Aye! The man-eater is dead-stabbed through the heart-and Conan is gone!"

Tarascus was gray of face as he mechanically allowed Orastes to force him prostrate again and the priest renewed work upon his mangled flesh.

"Conan!" he repeated. "Not a crushed corpse-escaped! Mitra! He is no man; but a devil himself! I thought Xaltotun was behind this wound. I see now. Gods and devils! It was Conan who stabbed me! Arideus!"

"Aye, your Majesty!"

"Search every nook in the palace. He may be skulking through the dark corridors now like a hungry tiger. Let no niche escape your scrutiny, and beware. It is not a civilized man you hunt, but a blood-mad barbarian whose strength and ferocity are those of a wild beast. Scour the palace-grounds and the city. Throw a cordon about the walls. If you find he has escaped from the city, as he may well do, take a troop of horsemen and follow him. Once past the walls it will be like hunting a wolf through the hills. But haste, and you may yet catch him."

"This is a matter which requires more than ordinary human wits," said Orastes. "Perhaps we should seek Xaltotun's advice."

"No!" exclaimed Tarascus violently. "Let the troopers pursue Conan and slay him. Xaltotun can hold no grudge against us if we kill a prisoner to prevent his escape."

"Well," said Orastes, "I am no Acheronian, but I am versed in some of the arts, and the control of certain spirits which have cloaked themselves in material substance. Perhaps I can aid you in this matter."

The fountain of Thrallos stood in a clustered ring of oaks beside the road a mile from the walls of the city. Its musical tinkle reached Conan's ears through the silence of the starlight. He drank deep of its icy stream, and then hurried southward toward a small, dense thicket he saw there. Rounding it, he saw a great white horse tied among the bushes. Heaving a deep gusty sigh he reached it with one stride-a mocking laugh brought him about, glaring.

A dully glinting, mail-clad figure moved out of the shadows into the starlight. This was no plumed and burnished palace guardsman. It was a tall man in morion and gray chain-mail-one of the Adventurers, a class of warriors peculiar to Nemedia; men who had not attained to the wealth and position of knighthood, or had fallen from that estate; hard-bitten fighters, dedicating their lives to war and adventure. They constituted a class of their own, sometimes commanding troops, but themselves accountable to no man but the king. Conan knew that he could have been discovered by no more dangerous a foeman.

A quick glance among the shadows convinced him that the man was alone, and he expanded his great chest slightly, digging his toes into the turf, as his thews coiled tensely.

"I was riding for Belverus on Amalric's business," said the Adventurer, advancing warily. The starlight was a long sheen on the great two-handed sword he bore naked in his hand. "A horse whinnied to mine from the thicket. I investigated and thought it strange a steed should be tethered here. I waited-and lo, I have caught a rare prize!"

The Adventurers lived by their swords.

"I know you," muttered the Nemedian. "You are Conan, king of Aquilonia. I thought I saw you die in the valley of the Valkia, but -- " Conan sprang as a dying tiger springs. Practised fighter though the Adventurer was, he did not realize the desperate quickness that lurks in barbaric sinews. He was caught off guard, his heavy sword half lifted. Before he could either strike or parry, the king's poniard sheathed itself in his throat, above the gorget, slanting downward into his heart. With a choked gurgle he reeled and went down, and Conan ruthlessly tore his blade free as his victim fell. The white horse snorted violently and shied at the sight and scent of blood on the sword.

Glaring down at his lifeless enemy, dripping poniard in hand, sweat glistening on his broad breast, Conan poised like a statue, listening intently. In the woods about there was no sound, save for the sleepy cheep of awakened birds. But in the city, a mile away, he heard the strident blare of a trumpet.

Hastily he bent over the fallen man. A few seconds' search convinced him that whatever message the man might have borne was intended to be conveyed by word of mouth. But he did not pause in his task. It was not many hours until dawn. A few minutes later the white horse was galloping westward along the white road, and the rider wore the gray mail of a Nemedian Adventurer.

Chapter 7

The Rending of the Veil

Conan knew his only chance of escape lay in speed. He did not even consider hiding somewhere near Belverus until the chase passed on; he was certain that the uncanny ally of Tarascus would be able to ferret him out. Besides, he was not one to skulk and hide; an open fight or an open chase, either suited his temperament bet-

ter. He had a long start, he knew. He would lead them a grinding race for the border.

Zenobia had chosen well to selecting the white horse. His speed, toughness and endurance were obvious. The girl knew weapons and horses, and, Conan reflected with some satisfaction, she knew men. He rode westward at a gait that ate up the miles.

It was a sleeping land through which he rode, past grove-sheltered villages and white-walled villas amid spacious fields and orchards that grew sparser as he fared westward. As the villages thinned, the land grew more rugged, and the keeps that frowned from eminences told of centuries of border war. But none rode down from those castles to challenge or halt him. The lords of the keeps were following the banner of Amalric; the pennons that were wont to wave over these towers were now floating over the Aquilonian plains.

When the last huddled village fell behind him, Conan left the road, which was beginning to bend toward the northwest, toward the distant passes. To keep to the road would mean to pass by border towers, still garrisoned with armed men who would not allow him to pass unquestioned. He knew there would be no patrols riding the border marches on either side, as to ordinary times, but there were those towers, and with dawn there would probably be cavalcades of returning soldiers with wounded men to ox-carts.

This road from Belverus was the only road that crossed the border for fifty miles from north to south. It followed a series of passes through the hills, and on either hand lay a wide expanse of a wild, sparsely inhabited mountains. He maintained his due westerly direction, intending to cross the border deep to the wilds of the hills that lay to the south of the passes. It was a shorter route, more arduous, but safer for a hunted fugitive. One man on a horse could traverse country an army would find impassable.

But at dawn he had not reached the hills; they were a long, low, blue rampart stretching along the horizon ahead of him. Here there were neither farms nor villages, no white-walled villas looming among clustering trees. The dawn wind stirred the tall stiff grass, and there was nothing but the long rolling swells of brown earth, covered with dry grass, and to the distance the gaunt walls of a stronghold on a low hill. Too many Aquilonian raiders had crossed the mountains in not too-distant days for the countryside to be thickly settled as it was farther to the east.

Dawn ran like a prairie fire across the grasslands, and high overhead sounded a weird crying as a straggling wedge of wild geese winged swiftly southward. In a grassy swale Conan halted and unsaddled his mount. Its sides were heaving, its coat plastered with sweat. He had pushed it unmercifully through the hours before dawn.

While it munched the brittle grass and rolled, he lay at the crest of the low slope, staring eastward. Far away to the northward he could see the road he had left, streaming like a white ribbon over a distant rise. No black dots moved along that glistening ribbon. There was no sign about the castle to the distance to indicate that the keepers had noticed the lone wayfarer.

An hour later the land still stretched bare. The only sign of life was a glint of steel on the far-off battlements, a raven to the sky that wheeled backward and forth, dipping and rising as if seeking something. Conan saddled and rode westward at a more leisurely gait.

As he topped the farther crest of the slope, a raucous screaming burst out over his head, and looking up, he saw the raven flapping high above him, cawing incessantly. As he rode on, it followed him, maintaining its position and making the morning hideous with its strident cries, heedless of his efforts to drive it away.

This kept up for hours, until Conan's teeth were on edge, and he felt that he would give half his kingdom to be allowed to wring that black neck.

"Devils of hell!" he roared to futile rage, shaking his mailed fist at the frantic bird. "Why do you harry me with your squawking? Begone, you black spawn of perdition, and peck for wheat to the farmers' fields!"

He was ascending the first pitch of the hills, and he seemed to hear an echo of the bird's clamor far behind him. Turning to his saddle, he presently made out another black dot hanging in the blue. Beyond that again he caught the glint of the afternoon sun on steel. That could mean only one thing: armed men. And they were not riding along the beaten road, which was out of his sight beyond the horizon. They were following him. His face grew grim and he shivered slightly as he stared at the raven that wheeled high above him.

"So it is more than the whim of a brainless beast?" he muttered. "Those riders cannot see you, spawn of hell; but the other bird can see you, and they can see him. You follow me, he follows you, and they follow him. Are you only a craftily trained feathered creature, or some devil in the form of a bird? Did Xaltotun set you on my trail? Are you Xaltotun?"

Only a strident screech answered him, a screech vibrating with harsh mockery.

Conan wasted no more breath on his dusky betrayer. Grimly he settled to the long grind of the hills, but dared not push the horse too hard; the rest he had allowed it had not been enough to freshen it. He was still far ahead of his pursuers, but they would cut down that lead steadily. It was almost a certainty that their horses were fresher than his, for they had undoubtedly changed mounts at that castle he had passed.

The going grew rougher, the scenery more rugged, steep grassy slopes pitching up to densely timbered mountainsides. Here, he knew, he might elude his hunters, but for that hellish bird that squalled incessantly above him. He could no longer see them in this broken country, but he was certain that they still followed him, guided unerringly by their feathered allies. That black shape became like a demoniac incubus, hounding him through measureless hells. The stones he hurled with a curse went wide or fell harmless, though in his youth he had felled hawks on the wing.

The horse was tiring fast. Conan recognized the grim finality of his position. He sensed an inexorable driving fate behind all this. He could not escape. He was as much a captive as he had been in the pits of Belverus. But he was no son of the Orient to yield passively to what seemed inevitable. If he could not escape, he would at least take some of his foes into eternity with him. He turned into a wide thicket of larches that masked a slope, looking for a place to turn at bay.

Then ahead of him there rang a strange, shrill scream, human yet weirdly timbred. An instant later he had pushed through a screen of branches, and saw the source of that eldritch cry. In a small glade below him four soldiers in Nemedian chain-mail were binding a noose about the neck of a gaunt old woman in peasant garb. A heap of fagots, bound with cord on the ground near by, showed what her occupation had been when surprized by these stragglers.

Conan felt slow fury swell his heart as he looked silently down and saw the ruffians dragging her toward a tree whose low-spreading branches were obviously intended to act as a gibbet. He had crossed the frontier an hour ago. He was standing on his own soil, watching the murder of one of his own subjects. The old woman was struggling with surprizing strength and energy, and as he watched, she lifted her head and voiced again the strange, weird, far-carrying call he had heard before. It was echoed as if in mockery by the raven flapping above the trees. The soldiers laughed roughly, and one struck her in the mouth.

Conan swung from his weary steed and dropped down the face of the rocks, landing with a clang of mail on the grass. The four men wheeled at the sound and drew their swords, gaping at the mailed giant who faced them, sword in hand.

Conan laughed harshly. His eyes were bleak as flint.

"Dogs!" he said without passion and without mercy. "Do Nemedian jackals set themselves up as executioners and hang my subjects at will? First you must take the head of their king. Here I stand, awaiting your lordly pleasure!"

The soldiers stared at him uncertainly as he strode toward

them.

"Who is this madman?" growled a bearded ruffian. "He wears Nemedian mail, but speaks with an Aquilonian accent."

"No matter," quoth another. "Cut him down, and then we'll hang the old hag."

And so saying he ran at Conan, lifting his sword. But before he could strike, the king's great blade lashed down, splitting helmet and skull. The man fell before him, but the others were hardy rogues. They gave tongue like wolves and surged about the lone figure in the gray mail, and the clamor and din of steel drowned the cries of the circling raven.

Conan did not shout. His eyes coals of blue fire and his lips smiling bleakly, he lashed right and left with his two-handed sword. For all his size he was quick as a cat on his feet, and he

was constantly in motion, presenting a moving target so that thrusts and swings cut empty air oftener than not. Yet when he struck he was perfectly balanced, and his blows fell with devastating power. Three of the four were down, dying in their own blood, and the fourth was bleeding from half a dozen wounds, stumbling in headlong retreat as he parried frantically, when Conan's spur caught in the surcoat of one of the fallen men.

The king stumbled, and before he could catch himself the Nemedian, with the frenzy of desperation, rushed him so savagely that Conan staggered and fell sprawling over the corpse. The Nemedian croaked in triumph and sprang forward, lifting his great sword with both hands over his right shoulder, as he braced his legs wide for the stroke-and then, over the prostrate king, something huge and hairy shot like a thunderbolt full on the soldier's breast, and his yelp of triumph changed to a shriek of death.

Conan, scrambling up, saw the man lying dead with his throat torn out, and a great gray wolf stood over him, head sunk as it smelt the blood that formed a pool on the grass.

The king turned as the old woman spoke to him. She stood straight and tall before him, and in spite of her ragged garb, her features, clear-cut and aquiline, and her keen black eyes, were not those of a common peasant woman. She called to the wolf and it trotted to her side like a great dog and rubbed its giant shoulder against her knee, while it gazed at Conan with great green lambent eyes. Absently she laid her hand upon its mighty neck, and so the two stood regarding the king of Aquilonia. He found their steady gaze disquieting, though there was no hostility in it.

"Men say King Conan died beneath the stones and dirt when the cliffs crumbled by Valkia," she said in a deep, strong, resonant voice.

"So they say," he growled. He was in no mood for controversy, and he thought of those armored riders who were pushing nearer

every moment. The raven above him cawed stridently, and he cast an involuntary glare upward, grinding his teeth in a spasm of nervous irritation.

Up on the ledge the white horse stood with drooping head. The old woman looked at it, and then at the raven; and then she lifted a strange weird cry as she had before. As if recognizing the call, the raven wheeled, suddenly mute, and raced eastward. But before it had got out of sight, the shadow of mighty wings fell across it. An eagle soared up from the tangle of trees, and rising above it, swooped and struck the black messenger to the earth. The strident voice of betrayal was stilled for ever.

"Crom!" muttered Conan, staring at the old woman. "Are you a magician, too?"

"I am Zelata," she said. "The people of the valleys call me a witch. Was that child of the night guiding armed men on your trail?"

"Aye." She did not seem to think the answer fantastic. "They cannot be far behind me."

"Lead your horse and follow me, King Conan," she said briefly.

Without comment he mounted the rocks and brought his horse down to the glade by a circuitous path. As he came he saw the eagle reappear, dropping lazily down from the sky, and rest an instant on Zelata's shoulder, spreading its great wings lightly so as not to crush her with its weight.

Without a word she led the way, the great wolf trotting at her side, the eagle soaring above her. Through deep thickets and along tortuous ledges poised over deep ravines she led him, and finally along a narrow precipice-edged path to a curious dwelling of stone, half hut, half cavern, beneath a cliff hidden among the gorges and crags. The eagle flew to the pinnacle of this cliff, and perched there like a motionless sentinel.

Still silent, Zelata stabled the horse in a near-by cave, with leaves and grass piled high for provender, and a tiny spring bubbling in the dim recesses.

In the hut she seated the king on a rude, hide-covered bench, and she herself sat upon a low stool before the tiny fireplace, while she made a fire of tamarisk chunks and prepared a frugal meal. The great wolf drowsed beside her, facing the fire, his huge head sunk on his paws, his ears twitching in his dreams.

"You do not fear to sit in the hut of a witch?" she asked, breaking her silence at last.

An impatient shrug of his gray-mailed shoulders was her guest's only reply. She gave into his hands a wooden dish heaped with dried fruits, cheese and barley bread, and a great pot of the heady upland beer, brewed from barley grown in the high valleys.

"I have found the brooding silence of the glens more pleasing than the babble of city streets," she said. "The children of the wild are kinder than the children of men." Her hand briefly stroked the ruff of the sleeping wolf. "My children were afar from me today, or I had not needed your sword, my king. They were coming at my call."

"What grudge had those Nemedian dogs against you?" Conan demanded.

"Skulkers from the invading army straggle all over the countryside, from the frontier to Tarantia," she answered. "The foolish villagers in the valleys told them that I had a store of gold hidden away, so as to divert their attentions from their villages. They demanded treasure from me, and my answers angered them. But neither skulkers nor the men who pursue you, nor any raven will find you here."

He shook his head, eating ravenously.

"I'm for Tarantia."

She shook her head.

"You thrust your head into the dragon's jaws. Best seek refuge abroad. The heart is gone from your kingdom."

"What do you mean?" he demanded. "Battles have been lost before, yet wars won. A kingdom is not lost by a single defeat."

"And you will go to Tarantia?"

"Aye. Prospero will be holding it against Amalric."

"Are you sure?"

"Hell's devils, woman!" he exclaimed wrathfully. "What else?"

She shook her head. "I feel that it is otherwise. Let us see. Not lightly is the veil rent; yet I will rend it a little, and show you your capital city."

Conan did not see what she cast upon the fire, but the wolf whimpered in his dreams, and a green smoke gathered and billowed up into the hut. And as he watched, the walls and ceiling of the hut seemed to widen, to grow remote and vanish, merging with infinite immensities; the smoke rolled about him, blotting out everything. And in it forms moved and faded, and stood out in startling clarity.

He stared at the familiar towers and streets of Tarantia, where a mob seethed and screamed, and at the same time he was somehow able to see the banners of Nemedia moving inexorably westward through the smoke and flame of a pillaged land. In the great square of Tarantia the frantic throng milled and yammered, screaming that the king was dead, that the barons were girding themselves to divide the land between them, and that the rule of a king, even of Valerius, was better than anarchy. Prospero, shining in his armor, rode among them, trying to pacify them, bidding them trust Count Trocero, urging them to man the wall and aid his knights in defending the city. They turned on him, shrieking with fear and unreasoning rage, howling that he was Trocero's butcher, a more evil foe than Amalric himself. Offal and stones were hurled at his knights.

A slight blurring of the picture, that might have denoted a passing of tune, and then Conan saw Prospero and his knights fil-

ing out of the gates and spurring southward. Behind him the city was in an uproar.

"Fools!" muttered Conan thickly. "Fools! Why could they not trust Prospero? Zelata, if you are making game of me, with some trickery -- "

"This has passed," answered Zelata imperturbably, though somberly. "It was the evening of the day that has passed when Prospero rode out of Tarantia, with the hosts of Amalric almost within sight. From the walls men saw the flame of their pillaging. So I read it in the smoke. At sunset the Nemedians rode into Tarantia, unopposed. Look! Even now, in the royal hall of Tarantia -- "

Abruptly Conan was looking into the great coronation hall. Valerius stood on the regal dais, clad in ermine robes, and Amalric, still in his dusty, blood-stained armor, placed a rich and gleaming circlet on his yellow locks-the crown of Aquilonia! The people cheered; long lines of steel-clad Nemedian warriors looked grimly on, and nobles long in disfavor at Conan's court strutted and swaggered with the emblem of Valerius on their sleeves.

"Crom!" It was an explosive imprecation from Conan's lips as he started up, his great fists clenched into hammers, his veins on his temples knotting, his features convulsed. "A Nemedian placing the crown of Aquilonia on that renegade-in the royal hall of Tarantia!"

As if dispelled by his violence, the smoke faded, and he saw Zelata's black eyes gleaming at him through the mist.

"You have seen-the people of your capital have forfeited the freedom you won for them by sweat and blood; they have sold themselves to the slavers and the butchers. They have shown that they do not trust their destiny. Can you rely upon them for the winning back of your kingdom?"

"They thought I was dead," he grunted, recovering some of his poise. "I have no son. Men can't be governed by a memory. What if the Nemedians have taken Tarantia? There still remain the provinces, the barons, and the people of the countrysides. Valerius has won an empty glory."

"You are stubborn, as befits a fighter. I cannot show you the future, I cannot show you all the past. Nay, I show you nothing. I merely make you see windows opened in the veil by powers unguessed. Would you look into the past for a clue of the present?"

"Aye." He seated himself abruptly.

Again the green smoke rose and billowed. Again images unfolded before him, this time alien and seemingly irrelevant. He saw great towering black walls, pedestals half hidden in the shadows upholding images of hideous, half-bestial gods. Men moved in the shadows, dark, wiry men, clad in red, silken loincloths. They were bearing a green jade sarcophagus along a gigantic black corridor. But before he could tell

much about what he saw, the scene shifted. He saw a cavern, dim, shadowy and haunted with a strange intangible horror. On an altar of black stone stood a curious golden vessel, shaped like the shell of a scallop. Into this cavern came some of the same dark, wiry men who had borne the mummy-case. They seized the golden vessel, and then the shadows swirled around them and what happened he could not say. But he saw a glimmer in a whorl of darkness, like a ball of living fire. Then the smoke was only smoke, drifting up from the fire of tamarisk chunks, thinning and fading.

"But what does this portend?" he demanded, bewildered. "What I saw in Tarantia I can understand. But what means this glimpse of Zamorian thieves sneaking through a subterranean temple of Set, in Stygia? And that cavern-I've never seen or heard of anything like it, in all my wanderings. If you can show me that much, these shreds of vision which mean nothing, disjointed, why can you not show me all that is to occur?"

Zelata stirred the fire without replying.

"These things are governed by immutable laws," she said at last. "I can not make you understand; I do not altogether understand myself, though I have sought wisdom in the silences of the high places for more years than I can remember. I cannot save you, though I would if I might. Man must, at last, work out his own salvation. Yet perhaps wisdom may come to me in dreams, and in the morn I may be able to give you the clue to the enigma."

"What enigma?" he demanded.

"The mystery that confronts you, whereby you have lost a kingdom," she answered. And then she spread a sheepskin upon the floor before the hearth. "Sleep," she said briefly. . Without a word he stretched himself upon it, and sank into restless but deep sleep through which phantoms moved silently and monstrous shapeless shadows crept. Once, limned against a purple sunless horizon, he saw the mighty walls and towers of a great city of such as rose nowhere on the waking earth he knew. Its colossal pylons and purple minarets lifted toward the stars, and over it, floating like a giant mirage, hovered the bearded countenance of the man Xaltotun.

Conan woke in the chill whiteness of early dawn, to see Zelata crouched beside the tiny fire. He had not awakened once in the night, and the sound of the great wolf leaving or entering should have roused him. Yet the wolf was there, beside the hearth, with its shaggy coat wet with dew, and with more than dew. Blood glistened wetly amid the thick fell, and there was a cut upon his shoulder.

Zelata nodded, without looking around, as if reading the thoughts of her royal guest.

"He has hunted before dawn, and red was the hunting. I think

the man who hunted a king will hunt no more, neither man nor beast."

Conan stared at the great beast with strange fascination as he moved to take the food Zelata offered him.

"When I come to my throne again I won't forget," he said briefly. "You've befriended me-by Crom, I can't remember when I've lain down and slept at the mercy of man or woman as I did last night. But what of the riddle you would read me this morn?"

A long silence ensued, in which the crackle of the tamarisks was loud on the hearth.

"Find the heart of your kingdom," she said at last. "There lies your defeat and your power. You fight more than mortal man. You will not press the throne again unless you find the heart of your kingdom."

"Do you mean the city of Tarantia?"

She shook her head. "I am but an oracle, through whose lips the gods speak. My lips are sealed by them lest I speak too much. You must find the heart of your kingdom. I can say no more. My lips are opened and sealed by the gods."

Dawn was still white on the peaks when Conan rode westward. A glance back showed him Zelata standing in the door of her hut, inscrutable as ever, the great wolf beside her.

A gray sky arched overhead, and a moaning wind was chill with a promise of winter. Brown leaves fluttered slowly down from the bare branches, sifting upon his mailed shoulders.

All day he pushed through the hills, avoiding roads and villages. Toward nightfall he began to drop down from the heights, tier by tier, and saw the broad plains of Aquilonia spread out beneath him.

Villages and farms lay close to the foot of the hills on the western side of the mountains for, for half a century, most of the raiding across the frontier had been done by the Aquilonians. But now only embers and ashes showed where farm huts and villas had stood.

In the gathering darkness Conan rode slowly on. There was little fear of discovery, which he dreaded from friend as well as from foe. The Nemedians had remembered old scores on their westward drive, and Valerius had made no attempt to restrain his allies. He did not count on winning the love of the common people. A vast swath of desolation had been cut through the country from the foothills westward. Conan cursed as he rode over blackened expanses that had been rich fields, and saw the gaunt gable-ends of burned houses jutting against the sky. He moved through an empty and deserted land, like a ghost out of a forgotten and outworn past.

The speed with which the army had traversed the land showed what little resistance it had encountered. Yet had Conan been leading his Aquilonians the invading army would have been forced

to buy every foot they gained with their blood. The bitter realization permeated his soul; he was not the representative of a dynasty. He was only a lone adventurer. Even the drop of dynastic blood Valerius boasted had more hold on the minds of men than the memory of Conan and the freedom and power he had given the kingdom.

No pursuers followed him down out of the hills. He watched for wandering or returning Nemedian troops, but met none. Skulkers gave him a wide path, supposing him to be one of the conquerors, what of his harness. Groves and rivers were far more plentiful on the western side of the mountains, and coverts for concealment were not lacking.

So he moved across the pillaged land, halting only to rest his horse, eating frugally of the food Zelata had given him, until, on a dawn when he lay hidden on a river bank where willows and oaks grew thickly, he glimpsed, afar, across the rolling plains dotted with rich groves, the blue and golden towers of Tarantia.

He was no longer in a deserted land, but one teeming with varied life. His progress thenceforth was slow and cautious, through thick woods and unfrequented byways. It was dusk when he reached the plantation of Servius Galannus.

To Be Continued...

PHENOMENAL STORIES
ZIRL & SONS PUBLISHERS

An Old-Fashioned Shooting

(Part 5 of 6)

By Richard H. Nilsen

Chapter 29
'Releese' Points'

"He's apparently a customer of ours and he never won the second-grade spelling bee."

Keene was sitting at the kitchen table with a new outside door, obviously not matching the decor, installed half an hour ago.

"Why a customer of yours?" I asked over coffee, after the police had left and with Nancy gone back to work at her paper. If "whoever" could find us here, with all the precautions we had taken, we might as well go "back to normal-as-possible, in public, in front of God and everybody." And having gotten a little "shocky" in the process, Nancy was aiming for as normal a routine as possible.

"Educated guess. He's one of our readers," Keene answered, not shy about having a second helping of bacon and eggs, even at 11 a.m. I couldn't blame him. His loner gun had come in handy. The blood had been cleaned up, Rant's paw attended to, the dead canine weighing in at nearly 100 pounds, but of obscure origin having been carted off by the police canine unit with an argument between the blues as to whether there was just a mix of dog gone wild there or whether the animal was half wolf. They were off to the vet's to settle that argument. And

I didn't have a scratch on me. Always a cause for celebration.

"These mast-head letters that were used to make your little love note are from an antiquated typeset not too many papers use. We, being the upholder of local gossip and who-did-what-to-whom for more than a hundred years, have to prove our link to history with an old Gothic Bookplate style that only reprints of 'Dracula' would use anymore. But at least it's distinctive enough to pick out in a line-up."

"Nice to hear you use 'we' instead of 'they' like you usually do when referring to the paper. Not that you've dropped your sarcastic tone, of course."

I had used Sherrill's FAX/photo machine to make a copy of the note before the cops took the original off for lab work. I didn't expect them to find much, though. After working with the police for some time, it becomes obvious that most criminals are stupid and in a state of emotional retardation at the time of their crime and their first foray into legal limbo gets them the maximum number of three-hots-and-a-cot in county correctional. How else would they be caught? The rarely used plea of "temporary insanity" overly quoted on TV should actually be "temporary stupidity."

Whether it was an "estranged significant other," inside job by a guy in hock up to his ears or somebody with an inflated insurance policy, culprits tend to volunteer their guilt by their actions and obvious motive.

In the rare cases where somebody is smart and not doing something obvious, the cops don't have a chance. I heard recently we were incarcerating the most prisoners in history in these United States, surpassed only by the number in Russian prisons. Ah yes, Mother Russia is again number one. China had us all beat with it's number of executions. So much for the thought of the day. Keene proceeded with his show and tell.

"See the way the lettering is a little cockeyed, but pretty even overall? Kind of like the guy who sets up his kids' "Veggies For Sale" sign with the 's' backwards to make it look cute. And 'releese' is such an obvious misspelling. I revise my original judgment to say that they want us to THINK they lost the second-grade spelling bee. They really won. At least by third grade."

"And they may want us to THINK the whole thing has to do with wolves and the park controversy?" I raised a mug of coffee to Keene in mock toast.

"Could be," Keene answered. "Or they could just be wolves in wolves' clothing."

"Ah, yes. Never pass up an opportunity to find the bad side of a person. Playing the percentages again, Keene?"

"You rarely go home broke betting on the total depravity of man."

"You and John Calvin. A couple of cut-ups."

But I was being swayed over to

Keene's view in spite of myself. Nothing like your old girlfriend getting the piss knocked out of her with you the most likely tag, your house getting burnt down, a couple of dead bodies and wild dogs or wolves set upon you to make you wonder about Mr. Rogers' view of nice people. Welcome to the neighborhood.

No wonder Nancy was finding solace back at her old beat. I was actually surprised she and Keene didn't act more like competitors, working for different papers. Keene's take was their clientele were too different to really compete. I think that meant Nancy's paper's readers were more than high school graduates and didn't have the comics as their most-read page. It also occurred to me that I didn't really know much about newspapers and reporters. Maybe their areas of coverage were so different, they didn't give a rat's ass about who covered what or who got credit for what. Maybe they weren't in competition at all.

"So you think somebody's trying to tag the local woodchucks for what somebody else, with more 'normal' motives has been doing?"

"Well," Keene said, "if I was caught doing something and wound up killing to cover it up, I'd point to someone else to take the blame in a heartbeat. No black humor intended."

"Yeah, but who did what to whom?"

"You mean before Mantham Jr. and the burnt carcass got their wagons derailed?"

"And my house burnt, my old girlfriend knocked around and Sherrill's house broken into with wolves set on..." Keene started laughing in the middle of my tirade.

"Oh, come on Hal, you stepped in shit and you know it! Your 'house' as you call it was a hermit's nightmare and the insurance paid out will give you the chance to make something decent. Your old girlfriend was a pain in the ass and somebody knocking her around did you a favor! She got punished and you don't even have to feel guilty! You got a new and miraculously better relationship out of it that you damn well don't deserve as far as I can see. And Sherrill's house damage is no skin off your nose the way he's insured! All this activity will be great publicity for your work and old man Mantham's paying you for the snooping you love to do anyway. You'd do it for free if he wasn't paying you! For once admit things are going your way instead of crying all the way to the bank!"

I hate it when Keene does this. When he's right he rubs it in unmercifully. But he seemed right enough this time. I tried to look appreciative.

"Speaking of the golden goose, I ought to call in and give him an update."

With that I left Keene to feel sorry for himself, and envious of me while also knowing I was just lucky and didn't deserve any of this which he would of course never get handed to him. He marinated in this kind of self pity and unfairness. It didn't get much better than this.

Chapter 30: Two Steps Back

Mantham Senior wasn't in, so I left a message. Actually I left an abbreviated report, figuring some info was better than just a "call me and I'll tell you what's going on" kind of message.

Personally, I hate that. If somebody leaves a message, leave a MESSAGE, not just directions to call back and play phone tag.

It's almost like email when you leave actual information. "Got your message. Yes to question number one. No to question number two. I'll be back at the phone around seven." Stuff like that. At least something has been communicated and it's not just a complete waste of time.

Everybody has a different opinion about time wasting. To me, lying in the sun is a waste of time and an invitation to melanoma. To Nancy, reading or working on a laptop in the shade under an umbrella while at the beach is a waste of R&R. Personally, I think 10 minutes in the tanning booth is about as much sensory deprived therapeutic down time as I can stand. Any more than that becomes work. But everybody's got an opinion. As a lady once told me, "That's why God invented chocolate and vanilla."

So here I was back, basically, to where I was before "they" burnt my house down. I still didn't have much of an edge on whether the culprits were pro or anti-tree hugging, garden variety criminals or police related psycho's who were seriously considering putting me six feet under as part of their cover-up.

I decided to give Philo Brown a call at dispatch. Philo was a black 911 officer in a predominately white force and county. He didn't exactly wear his color on his sleeve, but he was just opinionated enough to keep a watch out for his own backside, and that often meant knowing where the dirt was and who put it there. It reminded me of the corollary to the Serenity Prayer,

"God give me the street smarts to put up with all the shit most people complain about, complain about all the shit most people keep quiet about and the wisdom to bury the bodies of those who piss me off where nobody will ever find them."

I was kind of hoping our current perpetrators weren't especially adept at this same wisdom in their misdeeds. We'd found the bodies so far. But would we find the culprits?

Philo was off duty according to the 911 office. I called him at home and he agreed to meet me down at "News and Qs" off the Four Corners on South Main Street. It had been "The Main Street News" until it absorbed "The Q Billiard Parlor" next door for non-pay-

ment of rent. Now the place had the biggest variety of magazines in town, a dozen pool tables (let's face it, nobody plays "billiards" anymore), coffee, bagels, donuts and even flavored coffees, teas and soft drinks.

For those in the know, there

was a back stairs that one had to pass the register and go behind the counter to find. Liquor without benefit of license and dollar limit poker were played there far into the night and even through the night on weekends. Bets were also taken on various sports. All in all the place made much better money than it's disreputable exterior gave cause to suspect. The cops also were pretty sure numbers were being run out of the place. They were pretty sure, because many of the cops played those numbers. No need for payola when the local constabulary is part of the clientele.

Philo hadn't gotten there yet when I arrived, so I pumped a large cup of hazelnut coffee from an air-pot and racked up for a game of one man, call your pocket. Hazelnut nearly put me in the category of flaky coffee-boutique geeks, but I liked the change every so often.

Strange enough that News and Qs had it at all. I had just lucked out on a bank shot when Philo slipped in the side door.

We nodded and "hey'd" each other and I asked him what he wanted to drink.

"Thc good stuff upstairs, if it was a couple of hours later and I didn't have to go on duty tonight. Who'd you piss off bad enough to burn your house down, anyway?" Philo put the emphasis on the last syllable with a little up-tilt in his voice so that his last word sounded like it was starting a whole new question.

"Damn if I know. What do you want in the here and now?"

"You buyin'? I'll take a large Expresso with a honey wheat bagel and pimento cream cheese. And an apple Danish chaser."

Since they had all of the above, I guessed Philo had been here before.

"You come here often, big fella?"

"I'm the runner on Mondays. Coffee, donuts, numbers." I just shook my head as I went to the register. At least he wasn't shy about it.

When I came back with his food and drink, he'd started a game of eight ball.

"I'm solid. The one ball went down off the break. You're it."

I explained what was going on as I lined up the fourteen and missed a bank in the side pocket. The cue ball kissed the five up against the three in the corner so that Philo had a can't-miss combination in the corner.

"Hey! You bought me food! Who I gotta kill for you to throw the game at me too?" Philo laughed a high, wheezy laugh and downed the two solids without blinking.

"What's the scuttle at 911? Who's the perp most likely to knock off another local talent? Any cops got your vote? That kind of stuff."

"Anybody can tell you that! Why you askin' me?"

"Anybody wasn't available. C'mon Philo, give."

He took out the seven and nine.

He was killing me.

"I heard you already got the 411. Why you need me to repeat it by callin' 911?"

"Does anybody NOT know what I'm up to?"

"Some upper Mongolian monks haven't got phone lines in yet. Everybody else knows," Philo laughed his wheeze or wheezed his laugh, depending on how you saw it.

"So what do I do? Take out a classified for the guilty parties to come on in and the D.A. will do a deal in their favor?"

"Up to you man. I'd just stop pissing them off if I was you."

All in all, good advice. And good advice was always appreciated. It was just rarely used.

"I can't quite do that. Guess I'll just walk softly and carry a big Tazer gun."

"Better have it fully charged and set to 'Hurt Bad.' Anything less and Rant is off to the doggy orphanage. I'll let you know if I hear anything." With that he sunk the eight ball and got in his car to drive away.

I stood like a jerk watching him drive away and paid the time on the table. There I go beating up on myself again. Maybe I didn't look like a jerk. I just felt like one. There's a subtle difference.

Harry Carlton was behind the counter, unaccountably bald, barrel chested and "rotund." He'd only worked there for about thirty years. He took a week in Las Vegas and one in Atlantic City every year. Other than that, he lived and breathed the pool hall and newsstand.

"Good Hazelnet, Harry. You change brands?"

"Nahh. You just don't have your bottom-of-the-birdcage-morning-after mouth. People think things change. They don't. People change. They get worse." Harry the philosopher.

"What do you think about these murders, Harry? Mantham and Spivac? Any scuttlebut? Any theories?"

"I always got theories, Johnson. My theories I keep to myself." I hated being called by my last name. I felt like roll call in second grade. But Harry called everybody by their last name. As far as Harry keeping things to himself, that was a big lie. He was wanting me to beg a little. So I played along.

"But if you were to tell a guy who cared to listen, what would you say?"

"I'd say Mantham was screwing around with somebody and switched partners without permission. The guy has money up the kazoo with his family, so it's gotta be sex. Everything comes back to money, power and sex. The guy has money and power, therefore it's door number three."

"OK, and what about Spivac? He part of the sex thing, too?"

"Nahh! He knew too much. Jilted lover number one has to keep out of the dock. So he has to ice Spivac. Torch him, actually, with a fake deer thing up his ass."

"Antler. It was a deer antler. Also, not fake. Some people think

IMPERIAL ROADSTER (with rumble seat). $2895 at factory. Wire wheels extra.

ULTRA-FASHIONABLE

A New Imperial Custom Roadster

CONNOISSEURS of motor car beauty have accepted the new Chrysler Imperial as the most beautiful roadster on the road. It is self-evidently today's masterpiece of style and symmetry—a sports car different from all traditional designs. The new custom body is the finest expression of the sophisticated taste and masterly technique of Locke, who designed it. The sloping silhouette and the curve of the bas-relief modeling which sweeps with graceful flourish across the lower section of the body are new notes in roadster appearance—focal points of charm and distinction. The rumble seat compartment has a door on the curb side and a separate windshield, fitted, like the folding windshield in front, with non-shatterable glass. Beside this alluring newness of custom-body treatment, the new Imperial Roadster possesses that smooth, animated, sparkling performance which instantly typifies the masterful genius of Chrysler engineering. Price $2895 at the factory. Wire wheels extra.

CHRYSLER
IMPERIAL

it was to demonstrate the plight of deer in the Adirondacks if wolves are released into the wild. You know, like how'd you like to be gored by a deer antler if you're gonna' put wolves out where the deer herds are."

"And where the buffalo roam. My ass, Johnson. Wolves are to keep the deer herds from getting too big. The hunter's just want extra targets to shoot at. You want the murderers, look closer to home and forget the environmental pseudo-crapola."

I didn't want to agree with anything Harry had to say. Except I already thought the same thing. So I kind of had to agree with him. At least I thought of it first.

Chapter 31:
The Hard Way

I had a late lunch with Nancy at Lanzi's-on-the-Lake and we sat on the deck overlooking the docks. The lake level was still down this early in the season and so no boats were docked there yet. The rocks and driftwood-strewn beach stretched an extra fifty feet more out towards the water than usual, due to the low level. Every year the Black River and Hudson River Power Corporation regulated the Sacandaga River flow by way of a dam on the Sacandaga Reservoir. No one could actually own lakefront due to the power corporation's ownership and regulation of the surrounding area. Whatever they considered the "flood plain." You basically paid rental for use of the waterfront. "Beach rights" was what it was called, although rocky shoal rights would often be more accurate.

It was a weekday lunch-time and the place was pretty empty. Lanzi's often had parties and activities there, but we had lucked out on a "dead" day. One of the Lanzi brothers was always around. They probably only worked about 80 hours per week. And they always looked pleased as punch to see me, even though I usually ordered from the bar menu, so they sure weren't after my money.

Lou was here today. He'd put off building his new house on the lake to put all his efforts and capital into an expansion here and building another restaurant about six miles north of here near the bridge at Northville. It looked like the master plan was to have each of the five brothers eventually have his own restaurant.

"How you guys doing today? Got everything you need?" Lou asked, smiling like I was some long lost cousin who'd found his way home.

"Sure Lou, this is Nancy."

Greetings. Felicitations. He went on to the next table. I had jumbo shrimp the size of small pork chops. Nancy had a pasta salad and we split a platter of Mexicali Taco Salad.

Nancy was telling me about the job her editor had her on. Something about the school board member of a neighboring town voting for an office supplies

package that was later serviced through the school board member's paper company.

I was only half listening. Nancy was good to look at and you could say her looks drowned out her words. She probably would have found that offensive. Pretty girls always want to be taken more seriously. Smart girls would rather be beautiful. Everybody always wanted to be something different than they were. One of life's little lessons: Wherever you go, you are who you are. Or something like that.

As she talked an old limerick went through my head, "She offered her honor; he honored her offer. So all the night long he was on her and off her." It's crazy what goes through your head sometimes-or maybe not so crazy.

"Well, what do you think?" Nancy was looking at me like I should have been listening better. I cleared my throat, obviously stalling.

"More importantly, what do YOU think?" I answered, hoping to look sincere.

"I TOLD you what I think! Should I go with it?"

Should she, indeed?

"Go with your gut. When your head and heart argue, one should go with her heart. At least if they're talking about something they really care about." Once again, I was sincere as hell. I just wished I knew what I was talking about.

"You're right! I shouldn't go through a friend to get the goods on her father. Guess I'll have to dig up the dirt the hard way."

I was glad to be right about something, even if I didn't know what it was. Apparently there were only two possible choices. That was my first piece of luck. Next I had to pick the right one of the two. Lucky again. But then, it was fifty-fifty each time. You pay your money and you take your chance.

"You know, Nancy, your problem makes me think I need to come at my thing differently, too."

"How so?"

"Well, I've been riding the wave of being on the inside with the police and on-call people. Thought I could get a line on the possible killers that way. Thing is, they know too much about me. Everything travels in a big circle. I ask somebody about somebody and that somebody hears about it and it comes back on me."

"And what's the antidote for this?" Nancy said, her mouth full of taco salad.

"Same as with your story. I have to do it the hard way. I have an idea who a couple of possibles are. I just have to do the sit-in-the-car-and-watch-the-house stuff. Then the follow-their-car-and-stay-out-of-sight stuff. It's called detective work, and I've been avoiding it."

"Want somebody to ride shotgun with you?"

"Sure! We could pretend to neck in the car. In fact we could REALLY neck in the car and PRETEND to be doing surveillance. Of

course the cops in question might come up to the car and bust our chops just to be regular cop-like dudes and if they clue into what we're doing our bodies could be found in the spring on a mountain trail."

"I don't think so," Nancy said. "That's been done. And so far, these guys have not been redundant."

"OK. You've twisted my arm. Is it a date?"

"Sure! I'll bring the donuts and thermos of hot coffee."

"And I'll bring the night binoculars and mayonnaise jar to pee into." I answered.

She shook her head.

"The mayo jar thing doesn't work with us girls. We have to hold our knees together until an appropriate powder room becomes available. Speaking of which...." Nancy arose from the table and walked towards the rest rooms. I liked to watch her walk through the bar. Self-assured. Smiling. Time to shorten the sails and batten down the hatches. When you start smiling at the sight of someone and they don't know it and there's no one to show off to, it's like drinking alone. Addictive. Dangerous. Excess. Puritanical alarm bells go off in your head. "This is too good. This is too nice. I don't deserve this." That kind of crap.

When she came back I asked if she could swap with one of her co-workers' cars so it wouldn't be recognized. She made the arrangements and we got the car from the newspaper's parking lot. We drove to the Sheriff's Department and parked between the nursing service cars in the parking lot. Our county's Sheriff's Department was housed in the same building as the county nursing service and next door to the jail. Made things convenient. We faded into the background and waited for my "most likely to commit murder" candidates on the force to come out and go off shift. We didn't have long to wait.

Chapter 32:
Hot On the Trail

There's a major problem with tailing a police car. They are looking for suspicious looking vehicles. What's more suspicious looking than a car following a black and white? Besides, it stood to reason that anyone doing something wrong who were members of the sheriff's department wouldn't do it too obviously while on duty, in uniform, in a marked car. Of course, these are all thoughts that come to one after it's too late and such a foolish plan of action has already been kicked into gear.

Hines and Ballard came off duty while I was hardly into my second cup of coffee from Nancy's thermos. It had helped knowing when shift change was, but things happening according to schedule were still an unusual thing for me.

Nancy was driving the car she'd borrowed. We'd had the first small vestiges of a disagreement about who would drive. I've never been able to lie about getting carsick as a passenger like some say in order to be the driver. It's akin to arguing that I become disoriented if I don't possess the remote control while watching TV. Doesn't fly with anyone who has at least a two digit I.Q. Besides, she could look like an innocuous woman driver if spotted while I dropped below window level. And it would leave my gun arm free. That was her final argument. Now I knew how low she would stoop to get her way. It was disconcerting.

"They're apparently carpooling," Nancy remarked. "Maybe they're into the environmental thing after all."

"And maybe they're sharing the same bunk bed. And maybe they like to wear uniforms and guns out of civic pride and a patriotic spirit. And there's the great pumpkin to believe in."

Nancy turned to me clucking her tongue. "And they say reporters are jaded! Does that mean you WON'T wait with me at the pumpkin patch under a starry night so long ago foretold?"

Hines and Ballard apparently weren't in any hurry. They also apparently had a more conservative approach to the driver-passenger thing. Ballard climbed in the passenger side and then they just sat there a while.

"What do you think? Watching out for tails?" Nancy talked so low it was nearly a whisper.

"You mean people following or cruising for chicks?" I asked.

"Both of them into the female of the species?" Nancy asked casually.

"So I'm led to believe."

I tried to lower my voice a half octave and continued, "Kate's probably never met a real man who could satisfy...." We both started giggling uncontrollably at this point. Nerves, I guess.

Nancy sniffed and wiped her eyes, "Or maybe Hines needs to get in touch with his female side."

"You think the uniform helps with that?"

"God knows," she gasped. "You certainly have no clue."

"That's why they call me The Clueless Dick."

"Better than the other way round," she said. "I'll never forget the headline we ran when that guy lopped off his own member! We went round and round at editorial before they came up with 'Man cuts off own penis. Kind of no way to say it in a dignified or respectable manner."

"Ouch! Apparently it was a member in poor standing."

"And never will again... Ought-oh, I think they're moving out."

Hines car was slowly leaving thc drive. I started to caution Nancy to hang back, but she gave me such a withering look, I swallowed my words. She apparently didn't take instruction well.

The lights of his Camaro were easy to follow, anyway. He had some kind of grill work over the tail lights that left diagonal slits somewhat unmistakable from other cars. Not that there was much traffic along 29 west anyway. Good news; bad news. Easy to follow; hard to conceal our presence. We hung about a half mile back and found that Hines was very law abiding as far as speed went.

Route 29 west would eventually wind up in Saratoga Springs, but I didn't think that was where they were going. Sure enough they went north on Route 30 at Vails Mills, took a right and went through Broadalbin so slowly I thought I could get out and trot along side the car.

"What's this about?" Nancy asked.

"The cop in Broadalbin is especially protective of his turf and his super-slow speed limit. He'd love to give a deputy sheriff a ticket just to show how fair he is. To hell with professional courtesy and all that."

"I'll remember that."

We picked up speed north of Broadalbin and continued towards Fish House, avoiding Lakeview Drive. Fish House was established back when Sir William Johnson was Baronet here in colonial times. Fish House functioned back then as obviously as the name implied. When not stirring up his native American allies against the French, it was a place for Sir William to go fishing. We passed The Black Market, a cinder-hued flea market and pulled off at the sign for the Sacandaga Fish and Game Club. The past three miles had been a more winding road and Nancy had suitably shortened the gap so we wouldn't lose them at a sudden turn off.

"Well, well. This looks promising," I said. "A little obvious, but promising."

The drive to the Fish and Game was a winding, single lane. Any car coming down it would be pretty obvious, especially at this time of night, so we decided to pull off the other side of the road behind a Lilac Bush and go in on foot. I had a small Maglite that could focus to a pencil thin stream, a camera with 1,000-speed low-light film, a micro-cassette recorder and my borrowed .45. Nancy carried a shoulder bag with who knows what in it. Maybe a notebook in case she did an interview out here. The driveway was about a half-mile long, or at least it seemed so in the dark.

When we finally got to the main cabin, we found Hines' Camaro parked beside a couple of CJ-7 Jeeps, an old International Scout and a new Hummer that looked like an armored personnel carrier. The Camaro was strangely out of place here. And the armored personnel vehicle did not look like it was just for show. There was a nice thick coat of half-dried mud on the tracks and cowling.

"This must be the group's recreational vehicle for killing and pillaging. Kind of a modern-day Viking ship for fun and mayhem," I whispered in Nancy's ear.

"Bigger toys for bigger boys," Nancy answered. "But you are assuming a lot, aren't you? What if this is just a meeting for hunters and fishers like the sign says?"

"Then we start over, elsewhere. Let's go see if we can crash the party."

"You are kidding, I hope."

"A quiet crash. The kind of crash they won't know happened."

"Do you have your super snoop stuff with you?"

"My cassette recorder does have an amplified, directional mike. Not exactly state of the art. No 'Big Ear' snoop mike where you record from across the forest. I always thought that kind of took the challenge out of things."

"Translates as you couldn't afford it or didn't think you'd use it that much?"

"Bingo." All this was whispered back and forth from mouth to ear. The humor dissipates a little when whispering, but the accompanying nuzzling was nice.

We came up to the side of the building where a window was near a through-the-wall vent for a gas heater. Choosing between seeing and hearing (the vent was a pretty good ear into the interior), Nancy looked through the window while I put the recorder into use by the vent. I sneaked a look through the window first, though.

There were six figures in poor lighting around a circular table with long neck beer bottles all around. A vision of King Arthur's knights popped into my head unbidden. Either the drink menu was limited or somebody had brought the supplies and favored one brand. Hines and Ballard were there and out of uniform. I was trying to figure out how they had changed so fast, then realized they had gotten into the Camaro in civvies.

In the dim lighting I couldn't pick out the identity of anybody else. Then I paid more attention to the tape recorder at the vent.

A lot of the conversation was in low tones, people talking all at once or laughter for no particular reason I was aware of. But I perked up at a comment from a low bass voice.

"You know you owe me a dingo, Hines. You weren't supposed to lose one last night."

"If they were as all-fired vicious as you made them out to be, there'd be dead meat in that house instead of you complaining about me losing your half-breed mutant wolf," Hines answered.

Then the first voice came back, "Well, I didn't know you were out to kill anybody. I thought you were just wanting to put a scare into them. Nosy tree kissers are one thing. I don't think that Johnson is such a big tree hugger. I heard he lives in a cabin in the park, he's not one of the downstate do-gooders."

"Lived in a cabin," a different voice piped up. "And he works for a nosy downstate tree hugger. You didn't have a problem when you burned him out, did you?"

Now a feminine voice I took to be Ballard's broke in. "It doesn't matter where he lived. He works for Mantham, the dead prick's daddy and so we know where his ass is. Unless you all want to start kissing Albany's asses and paying to have holding tanks pumped and asking permission to shoot deer in your own woods and if and where you can shit by their leave, then what the hell else do you want to do?"

Everybody toned down at that point, which made it sound like Ballard was a leader of this group. Then one more voice rose above the rest.

"I still think you and the kid-prick were pretty close, Kate. And I don't think it's just wolves in your backyard you're talking about. I think he ditched you for some fag."

The silence and tension after that remark were thick. Then I heard a whack and a sigh from Nancy. By the time I got to the window, I saw a figure on the floor and Ballard standing over it. As I watched, she kicked the figure in the side and a groan escaped the man who then swiped her foot to one side and she went down in a thump. A ring formed around the two now so it was hard to see. I heard a "Shit!" from someone, then the first figure limped towards the door.

"Time to vacate," Nancy said, and we trotted over to the driveway and got behind a tree just as a guy burst through the front door with Ballard behind him. As we watched, the first guy turned and Ballard brought out a service pistol and shot him. It happened just that fast. No threats from her. No protests from him. Just a flash and bang and down he went. The shot echoed through the woods and everyone including Nancy and I turned to stone.

To Be Concluded...

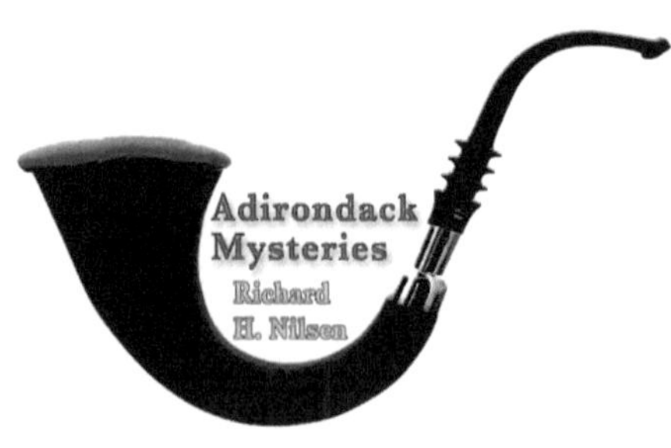

ZIRL & SONS PUBLISHERS

God Editor of Doom's Note: We start here the serialization of the only biography ever written about Robert W. Chambers. Chambers wrote 88 books and was one of the most published writers in the United States between roughly 1907 and 1930. Today, he is virtually forgotten because the novels he was most famous for then are seen now as quaint at best, terribly racist and sexist at worst. Now, Chambers is known largely for a single volume, The King in Yellow. It's intense, different type of horror – with a haunting beauty – influenced the writing of H.P. Lovecraft, Robert E. Howard, Clark Ashton Smith, Stephen King, Brian Lumley, Ramsey Campbell, Frank Belknap Long, Robert Bloch, E. Hoffman Price and many others. Despite his flaws, it is interesting to try to get a glimpse of who Robert W. Chambers was. That's what the author spent 37 years doing.

Robert W. Chambers: Maker of Moons

Author of The King in Yellow Unmasked

(Part 4)

By Shawn M. Tomlinson

Chapter 9

Country Life

Cardigan was an unusual serial in that it was spread across 27 weeks in a magazine not usually known for fiction. In fact, Harper's Weekly really is collected today only by people interested in its coverage of the American Civil War. The fact that it was printed on better quality paper than newspapers that covered the war makes it an easier item to find nearly 150

years after the event.

When collectors find the editions from 1901 these days, they routinely throw them out or cut them up for the advertisements that some people call art.

Collecting is a strange obsession, another of mine, but shared by many. It draws people toward a certain item or type of item to the exclusion of others. Collectors will search through ancient bookstores, barns, bins, wherever they think they might find the prized item.

Collecting Chambers' work is about average in difficulty. Since not a lot of people collect his works, when they are found, they rarely are that expensive. There are a few exceptions, of course, including the highest priced items like a first editions of *In the Quarter, With the Band* and especially *The King in Yellow*. Prices for these range from $250 for those in less than perfect condition all the way up to $2,000 or more for a first edition of *The King in Yellow*.

Yet *Cardigan*, his first real success, is readily available in a first edition for around $20.

If all one wants is to read the books, not find collectible copies such as first editions, most of them are readily available through AbeBooks.com and eBay in reprint editions, often for less than $10. For eBook editions, the price often is lower.

The Gutenberg Project has many of Chambers' books online available to read free of charge. See page 283 for a list.

At least at the turn of the century, Chambers didn't jump on the bandwagon of his success.

He had a bigger audience after *Cardigan*, but he spread his ideas around, not content to rewrite his historical fiction. He seemed to like spies and the one-person-saving-the-day scenario. He wrote pirate novels, war novels, spy novels, slightly paranormal stories and, of course, the so-called society novels that later would make him even more money and fame.

By 1901, Chambers had made himself lord of the manor in Broadalbin. Other rich people who lived there made their new homes a bit more modern. Chambers' house, redesigned and expanded by his architect brother, looks even today more like the White House, a building designed in the late 18th century.

Yet because of the waning fortunes of the Catholic Church in the United States in the 21st century, Chambers already diminished once-grand Broadalbin House has fallen to ruin.

For years after Father Peter Smith purchased the house and immediate grounds in 1954 — to use the house as a rectory and the front yard to build a church — the house remained vibrant and in use. The priests changed things around a bit, carving offices out of the large two-floor living room at the front, dropping the ceilings to cut heating costs, ripping out the statuary in the front yard for a parking lot, walling in the grand

Above: I led a tour of Chambers' estate and his gravesite in July 2008. The folks at the organization who arranged it must not have liked me very much because they never asked me to do it again, nor did any of them thank me. Oh well. Here I am talking with local historian, columnist and author Don Williams as we walk to the Chambers gravesite.

Below: Don and I stand at Chambers' family's section of the Broadalbin-Mayfield Rural Cemetery during the 2008 tour.

Photos by Gary W. Ziroli

staircase, again to save money on heat, and many other things, but they kept it painted and looking nice. It still was a showplace in Broadalbin until the last decade or so.

Then people dropped out of congregations. The Albany Diocese, which controls St. Joseph's in Broadalbin and thus the house, consolidated many churches, bringing several in each area under one priest. Some they closed. In the case of St. Joseph's, the diocese lumped it together with St. Francis in Northville 21 miles away. Because the St. Francis rectory was much more modest than Chambers' summer home, the lone priest was moved to that residence, leaving Broadalbin House mostly empty.

With the paint peeling off and the roof leaking, the diocese decided that by the end of the summer in 2014, the furniture would be auctioned off and either a buyer would need to be found or Chambers' home finally would be leveled.

That is today, however.

At the turn of the 20th century, all was bright and green in the hills and forests surrounding tiny Broadalbin, and Chambers and other rich people were making the most of it.

He chose — or perhaps listened to his architect brother — to rebuild the modest home of his grandfather into a pillared palace. It had none of that modern 1900 stuff, either, at least in the design. Instead, it resembled the White House.

Then, he dabbled. Outback, he had built a stone-and-timber Japanese teahouse, or at least what rich American high society members thought was a Japanese teahouse. It still stands, barely.

He also shared one design idea with Miss Kitty: They both had extensive and elaborate gardens built near their houses.

Husted had hers designed like Italian Gardens. They are called that still, although only a fragment remains. They had large wooden trellises, flower beds, arches and immaculately trimmed grass made just perfect for late Victorian, early Edwardian strolls on late summer afternoons.

Husted also had her own chapel, a small yellow building across the street from the great — and very modern — house built next to her family home on Maple Street. Chambers stayed in a nearby elaborate if small gray house while his own mansion was being refitted. That house still stands, too.

When it was finished, Chambers' large house stood at the end of a long, driveway. There were statues and paths around the house and in front stood a thick stone wall with wrought iron fencing on top. The caretaker's house was next door, beyond one wall, but still surrounded by the wall that kept it separate from the street.

It was behind the house that Chambers really went to work on his private playground.

Directly behind the house was

a large oak tree under which he originally was buried before being moved to the family crypt in the Broadalbin-Mayfield Rural Cemetery.

Behind the tree stands a small gardening shed and a walled path that leads up out of the gardens into the forest. There was a grand but rustic gazebo beside the path and white wooden gates that led into his sanctuary.

While I have no confirmation on the actual size of the estate, those who have known it said there were about 800 acres before the coming of the Great Sacandaga Lake in 1930.

The whole Sacandaga River Valley was forcibly abandoned in the 1920s through the eminent domain laws in New York state.

The problem was that severe flooding occurred downstream in the Albany area where many more people lived than in the rural Sacandaga Valley. This was caused by snow melt runoff into the Sacandaga River which flowed into the Hudson River. Various surveys and studies showed that placing a dam at Conklingville across the Sacandaga would control the flow of the river, but it would flood the valley. That meant all the farms and homes there would be destroyed. During the 1920s, the state bought all the property it was going to flood whether the inhabitants wanted to sell or not.

The Great Vlaie, along with villages and towns would be submerged. Part of Chambers' land, I believe, went under water, too, when the gates were closed at Conklingville March 27, 1930.

The part of Chambers' property that was above the new shoreline survived.

On those acres, he had rows upon rows of pine trees planted to repopulate the once-virgin forest. He had the small creek, Chambers Brook, dammed to create his own lake. On the southern edge of the shallow lake, he built a log cabin with a huge stone fireplace.

He had roads laid out through the woods and bridges built at several places along the way, all with the same dark stone that surrounds the estate.

The roads cut through the forest and led to a "V" that led down to the cabin.

In the small lake, Chambers fished the fish he had stocked there. He entertained special guests including, legend has it, Douglas Fairbanks and Mary Pickford.

Leon Crannell was his chauffeur and drove the big Packard through the forest on the dirt roads for his boss. He drove the same large car through the bustling streets of New York City.

The dirt roads still are there as are the bridges. Only the stone foundation of the cabin and the ever crumbling chimney still stand at the site of the cabin. The dam is broken in fragments in the water of the brook that now feeds the Great Sacandaga Lake.

Whether he voluntarily tore down his dam or it was taken by the Hudson River Regulating Dis-

trict is unclear. Kevin Ferguson, a surveyor for the organization now known as the Hudson River-Black River Regulating District, said the land was not seized from Chambers, but easements were granted.

The house, the grounds all began to fall into disrepair as the master died. His wife, Elsie, lived on at the great house for six more years, but when it passed into the hands of Robert Jr., the plunder of the old house really began.

Robert Jr., it was reported by many, rarely was at the house and left it unlocked. He was at least an alcoholic and possibly mentally unstable. John E. Boos, in *The Sacandaga Valley* published in 1962, told a story of a trip he took to meet Robert Jr., but found only the great open house. A boy told him he would find Robert Jr. in a bar.

Somewhere in the 1940s, a man named Griffith, a furniture dealer from nearby Amsterdam, took possession of the house. No one really is certain why or what he planned for the estate. It didn't matter. His fortunes fell and the house went back to Robert Jr.

The son loosely held the house until 1954 when he sold it and the surrounding property to the Albany Catholic Diocese in the care of Father Peter Smith who would take the house as the church rectory and build the stone church on the front corner.

The majority of the property went to local industrialist Arthur Chalmers who also had acquired Kitty Husted's home on Maple Street. Chalmers, who lived into his 100s, later gave the property to his doctor, Richard "Doc" Kearns, for keeping him alive so long, so the story goes.

Kearns kept the property relatively intact through the 1960s only finally allowing his daughter and her husband to build a house at the north end of Main Street just beyond Chambers' main gate in the late 1970s.

Later, a street was opened up what was known as the Bridal Path in my childhood to allow others to build homes there. It was paved and still ends at a dead end. It's called Dream Street. Beyond the light barrier there, the main original road from Chambers' time continues in its original form down the other side of the hill.

What was lost, however, is much. Chambers, along with his painting and writing, was a well-known entomologist who had one of the largest butterfly collections in the world. It was methodically catelogued and kept and added to most of his life.

According to my father, Robert M. Tomlinson, who was born in 1931 in Broadalbin, the collection was in the Broadalbin Elementary School for years, but kept in an unlocked case. It was destroyed, he said, by kids touching it, handling it, ruining it.

Along with this loss was the collection of historic letters from the likes of George Washington, the personal library that Chambers acquired over the years and a great number of paintings, both painted by him and by others that he admired.

The great white house is, in my mind, a bit like a very small version of the great library at Alexandria. That library held the wonders of the world, the largest collection of books ever assembled to that time. It was destroyed by peasants who burned it, tore it down as a symbol of empire.

The rule in Alexandria, according to the James Burke[1], was that any ship that docked there was required by law to loan any books it carried to the library for copying. At its height, this ancient library had in its collection most of the great plays of the Greeks, works of science, literature, mathematics, philosophy, essentially any book that can be imagined of the ancient world was there.

While Chambers did not own a collection nearly the size of that library, the analogy works because he did a great deal of research for his historical works. He collected letters and other documents of historical significance for this purpose. While he may have given up painting as a profession, he still painted and collected the works of others. He also collected books, both fiction and non-fiction.

What wonders would have been found glancing through the rooms, thumbing through the volumes, gazing at the paintings that lined the walls?

Like the library at Alexandria, we have only tantalizing fragments; a book here, a mention there, local tales of what happened, that's it.

And while his books give hints to the man, they don't give that many hints to the life he lived.

Still, I dig on.

References

1. Burke, J. (1978) *Connections*: Episode 2: Death in the Morning. Beers & Co., New York

Time: Book 2: Nemesis

continued from page 41

The popups weren't like tents, really. She didn't know how they were made, but once erected, she could stand inside and there was a bed and a toilet and shower in a separate section. She'd been in one briefly before, in Utah, when she first encountered Ted and his troops.

They blended into whatever terrain where they were setup, she knew. A soldier had explained to her that the entire outside surface was made up of, basically, tiny LCD screens and little cameras. The cameras caught whatever was around the popup and projected it onto the screens. Once closed, a popup was virtually undetectable until a person got to within 10 feet.

The soldiers used the same technology in their camouflage netting, which they strung above the desert-colored vehicles.

Chloe went inside the popup she shared with Martin to lie down while the work progressed. She knew they usually were in danger out in the open country wherever they went, but she did like traveling with Martin.

Not with Alex, of course, so this trip was a little different.

She could hear Alex and Martin talking outside, but decided it didn't matter right then. She was tired and, she told herself, lying down a few minutes would rest her.

Chloe woke with a start when Martin sat down on the bed beside her.

"Calm, calm," he said, brushing a hand through her soft hair. "It's good that you slept a little. The orderlies are bringing us dinner in a few minutes, so I wanted — but didn't want — to wake you."

He started to get up, but Chloe grabbed him and pulled him down half on top of her. She wrapped her arms tightly around him, smiled seductively and kissed him with an intensity he loved.

The table seemed an oddity, as did the chairs. Somehow, she thought they'd be sitting on rocks and eating rough.

Alex already was seated and had started without them.

Chloe and Martin took their seats and enjoyed the field cooking of the army chefs.

"We should make Twin Lakes by tomorrow afternoon," Alex said. "Major Briggs wants us to stay there for the night, even though we'll be there early. He said the scouts haven't spotted the prisoners yet, and they've gone as far west as Grand Junction, the last city before the state border. Briggs said he wants to enter Avon as early as possible so that we can get the lay of the land and set up and ambush for Shaw's men, free the prisoners."

"Reasonable," Martin said. "Any reason we aren't just pressing on to Grand Junction? It seems like we'd

Drink
NEHI

reach them sooner, save some more lives."

"True, but Ted ordered Briggs to Avon because, at least on satellite images of old, the place looks better militarily," Alex said. "Briggs thinks Avon is the spot, too."

Martin asked a soldier to bring him the satellite map after they finished their meal.

The three stood over it, looking intently at it when Major Briggs came over to them.

"General, if you have a better idea, of course we will follow your orders," he said stiffly.

"Not trying to ruffle feathers, major," Martin said, "just trying to see if there's a way for us to intercept these folks sooner. My guess is that many of them have died on the march already, and I'd like to limit the casualties. I think that Ted probably picked Avon because he believed the prisoner column would be closer to us by the time we got there. That doesn't appear to be the case, so I'm just wondering if we can take the war to their overlords sooner."

"The problem with Grand Junction, Sir, is that it still has a sizable population," Briggs said. "If any of them are loyal to Shaw, word could get to him about any ambush we might stage. That could make him nervous and he may put his people on high alert."

"That could put Jebba, Trevor and Alan in danger," Chloe said.

"OK, good points," Martin said, still looking at the map.

Chloe could see that look. Martin was rapidly weighing all the possibilities he could think of. She knew he'd figure something out.

"Major, here's a thought, and tell me if it's doable," Martin said after studying the map for some time. "What if we follow our original route along 25 here, then turn west on Route 285 instead of continuing north. Your worries about Shaw loyalists spotting us are valid, and the possibilities become probabilities the closer we get to Cheyenne Mountain, especially along a still-used road.

"So, OK, we go west on 285 to Saguache, then follow Route 114 west to 50, then north on 92 'til we get to Route 65 north," Martin said, drawing his finger along his suggested route. "This will get us to De Beque, which looks like a very small town just east and north of Grand Junction. We let Shaw's pigs lead the prisoners through Grand Junction along Interstate 70. It runs just south of De Beque, outside of the population center — if there is a population — and it looks like a fairly narrow canyon. We could wait until they get inside the area of the highway interchange, then take out the guards fairly easily and from good cover."

Briggs looked over the map carefully, considered thoughtfully, then said, "General, I think we can do it. The roads likely will be tougher to navigate, though, so it may take more time."

"You said your scouts put the prisoner column far west of Grand Junction," Alex said. "How long to they estimate until they reach that city?"

"Probably a week or more," Briggs said. "The general is correct: the conditions are dropping the prisoners daily. They started with about 500 prisoners and it looks like they're down to around 250 or so already."

Briggs turned to Martin, said, "You're right, General. We need to save as many as we can. We'll take your route in the morning."

"Thank you, major," Martin said, and Briggs returned to his troops to tell them about the change.

Martin cleared the table of the map, pushed his chair a bit back and Chloe sat on his lap.

Alex looked at them, said, "Oh, for God's sake, get a popup!"

She turned and went to her own.

Martin and Chloe laughed, kissed, and followed Alex's advice.

Chapter 13

Gen. Trevor O'Leary stood in front of his retinue with Col. Alan Burnside and Major Jessica O'Donnell at his sides.

Aside from Trevor, Alan and "Jessica" Jebba, there were a dozen men and women, soldiers trained as diplomatic guards. They were regular soldiers, but each had specialized training focused upon the intricacies of negotiations and negotiating teams.

There also was a young woman, Sophia Johnson, who was to act as the general's secretary. She was trained in special ops and held the rank of major, but she wasn't in soldier's garb for this mission. She wore what she told them had been "business casual" in an earlier Time.

Sophia looked the perfect secretary for Trevor. She was pretty, smart, wore glasses — for show; she usually used contact lenses — and fit him perfectly. After some drills together, she could anticipate his needs immediately, or even before he knew them. She fit the team well, as long as the other soldiers didn't salute her.

That had happened a few times, even when she was dressed as she was now. Jebba discovered that Sophia was a strict disciplinarian and took her rank very seriously. She had reprimanded many soldiers who failed to salute, and even many who didn't do it as fast or as efficiently as she demanded.

She knew all the soldiers in the group, so, with Trevor's permission, she stepped forward and they automatically snapped back to attention from their at-ease stances.

"Soldiers!" she barked, then softened a little. "That is the last time you will snap to attention for me... until after this mission. You all know what a pain I can be, but I am not in uniform now and undercover.

"Giving me a salute or coming to attention could jeopardize the mission and get any or all of us killed. For the duration, you will treat me with respect, but the same respect you give a normal civilian. I promise you, there will be no retribution afterward. We are a team, with each of us in our parts. Good luck to us all."

She stepped back to a place just behind General O'Leary.

He said to the retinue, "We all know I'm not a real general, not even a real soldier like you folks. But it is crucial for us to all act like

I am for the entire mission, from the time we leave the bunker through to being inside the lion's den and back out again. I will do my best to not disgrace us, and I thank you from my heart for your help."

A captain, this one in uniform, named Madison Strete, officially was in charge of the soldiers. She stepped forward toward Trevor, saluted, then turned back to the soldiers.

"Mount up!" she barked. "Let's move."

She led the troop out to the lift and they rode up to the little hut that served as a façade for the bunker.

Trevor, Jebba, Alan, Sophia and their driver, Kevin, boarded a Humvee with three-star flags at the fenders. Kevin kicked the vehicle to life and drove up the long, wide ramp to surface in the desert. The other vehicles, carrying the retinue, were driving toward them as they came through the ground. Capt. Strete's vehicle maneuvered in front of Trevor's and the others followed behind.

Although the vehicles were armored, they didn't have any extra weapons — other than a top-mounted machine gun on each — except Trevor's. While they could not be seen to be a threat, they also could not strip the vehicles of everything or they would appear weak.

Protocol said they could and must carry sidearms when accompanying a general, but assault rifles and other more useful weapons had to be locked in the vehicles upon entry to Shaw's mountain.

Kevin carried a sidearm, of course, and had access to two sawed-off shotguns under the dash.

Sophia sat beside him feeling a little uncomfortable without her sidearm. Behind them sat Trevor and Alan. Two more seats had been installed behind them. Jebba occupied one of them. The other held a briefcase filled with documents to make it look as though Trevor really was on a diplomatic mission.

He was, kind-of, speaking for the Eastern Power, but he doubted any "deal" he made would be honored by either side. He knew the only solution, even if nobody said it: Shaw had to be removed.

Trevor smiled as he remembered Martin referred to the rogue general as "Terence Effing Shaw" when he briefed the former about the crazy dictator.

"He's a weasel, at best, but weasels can be dangerous," Martin had said. "His deep bloodshot eyes told me even then that he was too paranoid to sleep. Terence Effing Shaw will stare at you while you talk, but he's not listening. Somewhere he learned that he has to appear to be listening, but all the time you talk, he'll just be thinking about what he has to say... and what horrible things he may want to do to you."

"Doesn't sound very nice," Burnside said.

"How'd he get to be general?" Trevor asked.

"Not sure," Martin said. "He already had that rank when I met him. He was the lowest form — in more than one way — of general he could be. My guess, and it's only a guess, is that after or during The Fall, Gen. Ramirez needed more top officers to keep discipline at the Mountain. Shaw probably had lied and blackmailed his way to being a colonel by then, so Ramirez probably had no choice. I think Shaw would have killed him no matter what happened, so it doesn't really make a difference.

"I think that if Gen. Thompson wanted to keep control after Ramirez' death, he couldn't remove Shaw. If he had, everyone would have questioned the whole structure. They weren't taking orders from Washington anymore, so it was important to keep to military structure as much as possible.

"I know Thompson didn't like Shaw, neither did Ramirez. I think that if we could have tied Ramirez' assassination to Shaw, then Thompson would have had him shot and this wouldn't be happening now. We couldn't and Shaw had a rabid, loyal band of followers, so he got to move up to second in command. It only took a well-placed bullet for him to move up again.

"Personally, I'd have taken him out for a smoke after the investigation and put 15 shots between his eyes," Martin said.

"Martin!" Chloe said. "You hate killing people!"

"Would have made an exception for Terence Effing Shaw," Martin said. "Bloody, sneaky, bastard. And now, of course, I wish I'd done it anyway. Probably would have had a reason to stage a trial for me then, but we wouldn't be in this mess now."

"OK, so your advice is to shoot him between the eyes as soon as we meet him?" Trevor asked, amused.

"Not a good idea," Martin said. "Remember his minions. Most of the people there probably hate Shaw, but his personal praetorian guard will have you ground up for dog food quick as hell if you even try to take a shot at Shaw."

"So what should we do?" Burnside asked.

"Follow Ted's plan," Martin answered. "Talk to him, express the Powers That Be's gentle displeasure with him, get him to assure you he won't invade Poland and then make him a tentative deal, telling him you have to consult with the leadership back East before anything can be in concrete."

"Invade Poland?" Chloe asked.

"Shaw is Hitler in this scenario," Martin said. "Chamberlain – Gen. Trevor O'Leary – appeased Hitler, let him keep his war machine and let him take territories he had no right to in exchange for Hitler's promise not to start a war. Short time later, Hitler invades Poland thinkin' the British are pansies, and World War II begins."

"Yikes!" Jebba said.

"That's what this minor mountain madman dictator is," Martin said. "So watch it.

"What else can you tell us about Shaw?" Burnside asked. "He seems like a monster from what everyone is saying, but there must be more to him than that."

"True," Jebba said, "even Hitler liked dogs."

"Very squirrelly," Martin said. "I interviewed him myself when we were talking to anyone who

might have known anything about Ramirez' murder. We sat down opposite each other across his desk in his office. I wanted him to feel in control and comfortable because I reasoned it was the best way to get him to open a little.

"He answered my questions, but said very little otherwise. What he said wasn't so important anyway. I was watching him, trying to get a sense of the man.

"During the interview and pretty much all the time, Shaw acted nervous and restless, as if he had to move all the time and might bolt out of his office... or lunge across his desk at me. I know he had his hand on a gun under his desk that was pointed at me during our talk."

"Didn't you think he was going to shoot you?" Chloe asked.

"Sure, but he's difficult to predict," Martin said. "I was ready to move if those rat bloodshot eyes twitched the wrong way. He twitched a lot, but didn't fire. I guess even he could realize that there would be no way out of getting caught for killing me. If he had, Thompson would have had enough to execute Shaw.

"Anyway," Martin went on, "the only time I ever saw him lighten up a little was when Alex was around him. She made a big point of finding him terribly handsome and virile. He actually smiled once, and he ever blinked a few times."

"So why didn't she do the interview with him?" Burnside asked.

"He would have seen her attentions as a ploy and killed her somehow," Martin said. "It was better that she kept her 'sincere' attentions on him and never appeared as a threat. It was Alex who kept him occupied enough for the rest of us to get a bead on his loyalists. If she hadn't distracted Shaw, he'd have gotten in our way a lot more and we never would have found the four who actually killed Ramirez.

"We all knew, though, that Shaw was behind it, just couldn't prove it. We warned Thompson and he must have listened for a while, but he slipped up and got dead."

"What should we watch for in this Shaw?" Burnside asked again.

"Hard to tell ya, Alan," Martin said, turning to him. "Follow your gut. Never trust him, of course, but you're great at talking to and wooing people, so just let the ol' Burnside charm do its work.

"It should be relatively easy, Trevor, to let Alan take the lead in negotiations and talks. You will have the final say, Shaw will expect that. But, you can indicate that Alan is your top advisor and best diplomat and that you would prefer to let him take the lead.

"Shaw's unpredictable, though, so he may not like that and insist upon only speaking directly to you, Trevor. If that happens, let it. Go with the flow. You're really good at negotiating those twists and turns."

"If Alex was so good with Shaw, if he liked her that much, why isn't she going inside with them?" Chloe asked.

Alex spoke up for the first time, said, "We had a bit of a falling out near the end of my time there."

"Figures," Chloe said quietly.

Alex ignored her, said, "It wasn't my doing. Gen. Thompson was trying to fix me up with his brother, a Col. Lazlo Thompson, so he arranged for me to sit with Lazlo at the farewell dinner. I had been sitting with Shaw whenever possible up until then, so he took it as a slight. He didn't speak to me again and I got the feeling I didn't want to be alone with him."

"He may take a liking to Jebba," Burnside said, casting a glance at her.

Jebba snort-laughed, said, "He better watch his nuts if he does."

"Or for that young major, Sophia, who is going as Trevor's secretary," Burnside went on. "She is very pretty and young, and she looks a little like Alex."

"Use that if you can," Martin said. "Warn her, explain it to her, but she can handle herself, I'd bet. She's special ops."

"I will do that," Trevor said. "Thanks for the briefing. We'll see you tomorrow."

Chloe, Martin and Alex left them to their drills and dress rehearsal.

Alex said goodbye to the two, then departed for her quarters.

As Chloe and Martin were about to leave the bunker, a soldier stopped them. He handed them a message from Ted. It said that they needed to leave early the next morning.

Trevor turned to look forward at Sophia. He had explained the plan to

her, but as tough as the girl seemed, he sensed vulnerability there. He wondered if she really could handle Shaw.

Kevin drove them north along Route 25, but had to turn east at Pueblo so they could head northwest to catch Interstate 70.

Ted had said they needed to appear to be coming from the east, so they couldn't take the direct route up 25. Instead, they had to travel much rougher roads out nearly to the Kansas border. It was going to be a long trip.

To Be Continued...

The Blue Wizard

continued from page 31

dipping here." Muttered Korvus.

"You don't have much of anything they want anyway." Intef snickered.

"More than you!," rejoined Korvus, waggling a pinky finger at him.

Intef leaned toward Sarafina and husked: "Like a baby's arm with an apple in its fist." And winked, she blushed to the roots of her hair and turned away. Koino turned her head, Nîlo darted a glance to see if it was true.

Intef caught him and smiled a knowing smile. Nîlo blushed and looked away.

Overhead the sea birds shrieked and circled as they approached the furthest out of the fishing boats. The fishermen waved as they passed, the company waved back. By now Intef and Korvus were rowing again. And making good time. As the sun was setting the sky and waters ablaze with brilliant reds, gold and oranges, they beached their craft and clambered out onto the white sands.

A small group of five people approached bearing the sigil of a blue bird wing on a white background. They wore blue feathers in their hair and two of them carried blue parrots on their shoulders.

"Welcome to Avaälun, our master Gylyf Betullu, the Beak in the Birches, the Master of Air and Water, bids you greetings."

"You knew we were coming?" Koino asked.

"The master knows many things, sees many things from afar. I am Aefon Pedero, Castellan of Avaälun, these are my assistants, allow us to escort you to the Keep where you may rest from your journey and refresh yourselves." He clapped his hands and several porters bearing litters approached.

"Climb in, climb in, it's a long walk in the hot sun if you don't!" He climbed into large litter, and was joined by one of his companions; they were carried by six burley men.

The rest got into to individual litters carried by two to four men each.

"As soon as everyone is settled," the Castellan said, "we'll be off." And so they were.

"I could get used to this." Intef chortled. "Hey, Nîlo, wanna share my litter?"

"No thanks, mine is fine." Nîlo deliberately looked the other way.

"Suit yourself." Relaxing with his hands behind his head, it wasn't long before Intef drifted off and was softly snoring.

To Be Concluded...

ZIRL & SONS PUBLISHERS

God Editor of Doom's Note: For various reasons, a lot of great stories have entered the Public Domain. That means anyone can use them without permission or payment to the estate of the author. I should feel guilty about using such stories, but so many pieces of my writing have ended up being stolen and printed without my permission or payment to me that I no longer do. So, we have the opportunity to present some great early works by some fantastic authors in Phenomenal Stories. The Girl in the Golden Atoms is one of those way pre-Golden Age stories that has at least a passing resemblance to H.G. Wells' War of the Worlds, but then again, so did most SF at the time. Either to Wells' work or that of Jules Verne. It's dated now, but a lot of fun. This novel was reprinted often, even in the early days.

The Girl in the Golden Atom

By Ray Cummings

[Part 3]

Chapter VI
Strategy & Kisses

"It was the morning of my third day in the castle," began the Chemist again, "that I was taken by Lylda before the king. We found him seated alone in a little anteroom, overlooking a large courtyard, which we could see was crowded with an expectant, waiting throng. I must explain to you now, that I was considered by Lylda somewhat in the light of a Messiah, come to save her nation from the destruction that threatened it.

"She believed me a supernatural being, which, indeed, if you come to think of it, gentlemen, is exactly what I was. I tried to tell her something of myself and the world I had come from, but the difficulties of language and her smiling insistence and faith in her own conception of me, soon caused me to desist. Thereafter I let her have her own way, and did not attempt any explanation again for some time.

"For several weeks before Lylda found me sleeping by the river's edge, she had made almost a daily pilgrimage to that vicinity. A maidenly premonition, a feeling that had first come to her several years before, told her of my coming, and her father's knowledge and scientific beliefs had led her to the outer surface of the world as the direction in which to look. A curious circumstance, gentlemen, lies in the fact that Lylda clearly remembered the occasion when this first premonition came to her. And in the telling, she described graphically the scene in the cave, where I saw her through the microscope."

The Chemist paused an instant and then resumed.

"When we entered the presence of the king, he greeted me quietly, and made me sit by his side, while Lylda knelt on the floor at our feet. The king impressed me as a man about fifty years of age. He was smooth-shaven, with black, wavy hair, reaching his shoulders. He was dressed in the usual tunic, the upper part of his body covered by a quite similar garment, ornamented with a variety of metal objects. His feet were protected with a sort of buskin; at his side hung a crude-looking metal spear.

"The conversation that followed my entrance, lasted perhaps 15 minutes. Lylda interpreted for us as well as she could, though I must confess we were all three at times completely at a loss. But Lylda's bright, intelligent little face, and the resourcefulness of her gestures, always managed somehow to convey her meaning. The charm and grace of her manner, all during the talk, her winsomeness, and the almost spiritual kindness and tenderness that characterized her, made me feel that she embodied all those qualities with which we of this earth idealize our own womanhood.

"I found myself falling steadily under the spell of her beauty, until – well, gentlemen, it's childish for me to enlarge upon this side of my adventure, you know; but – Lylda means everything to me now, and I'm going back for her just as soon as I possibly can."

"Bully for you!" cried the Very Young Man. "Why didn't you bring her with you this time?"

"Let him tell it his own way," remonstrated the Doctor. The Very Young Man subsided with a sigh.

"During our talk," resumed the Chemist, "I learned from the king that Lylda had promised him my assistance in overcoming the enemies that threatened his country. He smilingly told me that our charming little interpreter had assured him I would be able to do this. Lylda's blushing face, as she conveyed this meaning to me, was so thoroughly captivating, that before I knew it, and quite without meaning to, I pulled her up towards me and kissed her.

"The king was more surprised by far than Lylda, at this extraordinary behavior. Obviously neither of them had understood what a kiss meant, although Lylda, by her manner evidently comprehended pretty thoroughly.

"I told them then, as simply as possible to enable Lylda to get my meaning, that I could, and would gladly aid in their war. I explained then, that I had the power to change my stature, and could make myself grow very large or very small in a short space of time.

"This, as Lylda evidently told it to him, seemed quite beyond the king's understanding. He comprehended finally, or at least he agreed to believe my statement.

"This led to the consideration of practical questions of how I was to proceed in their war. I had not considered any details before, but now they appeared of the utmost simplicity. All I had to do was to make myself a hundred or two hundred feet high, walk out to the battle-lines, and scatter the opposing army like a set of small boys' playthings."

"What a quaint idea!" said the Banker. "A modern 'Gulliver.'"

The Chemist did not heed this interruption.

"Then like three children we plunged into a discussion of exactly how I was to perform these wonders, the king laughing heartily as we pictured the attack on my tiny enemies.

"He then asked me how I expected to accomplish this change of size, and

I very briefly told him of our larger world, and the manner in which I

had come from it into his. Then I showed the drugs that I still carried

carefully strapped to me. This seemed definitely to convince the king of

my sincerity. He rose abruptly to his feet, and strode through a doorway

on to a small balcony overlooking the courtyard below.

"As he stepped out into the view of the people, a great cheer arose. He waited quietly for them to stop, and then raised his hand and began speaking. Lylda and I stood hand in hand in the shadow of the doorway, out of sight of the crowd, but with it and the entire courtyard plainly in our view.

"It was a quadrangular enclosure, formed by the four sides of the palace, perhaps three hundred feet across, packed solidly now with people of both sexes, the gleaming whiteness of the upper parts of their bodies, and their upturned faces, making a striking picture.

"For perhaps ten minutes the king spoke steadily, save when he was interrupted by applause. Then he stopped abruptly and, turning, pulled Lylda and me out upon the balcony. The enthusiasm of the crowd doubled at our appearance.

I was pushed forward to the balcony rail, where I bowed to the cheering throng.

"Just after I left the king's balcony, I met Lylda's father. He was a kindly-faced old gentleman, and took a great interest in me and my story. He it was who told me about the physical conformation of his world, and he seemed to comprehend my explanation of mine.

"That night it rained — a heavy, torrential downpour, such as we have in the tropics. Lylda and I had been talking for some time, and, I must confess, I had been making love to her ardently. I broached now the principal object of my entrance into her world, and, with an eloquence I did not believe I possessed, I pictured the wonders of our own great earth above, begging her to come back with me and live out her life with mine.

"Much of what I said, she probably did not understand, but the main facts were intelligible without question. She listened quietly. When I had finished, and waited for her decision, she reached slowly out and clutched my shoulders, awkwardly making as if to kiss me. In an instant she was in my arms, with a low, happy little cry."

Chapter VII
A Modern Gulliver

"The clattering fall of rain brought us to ourselves. Rising to her feet, Lylda pulled me over to the window-opening, and together we stood and looked out into the night. The scene before us was beautiful, with a weirdness almost impossible to describe. It was as bright as I had ever seen this world, for even though heavy clouds hung overhead, the light from the stars was never more than a negligible quantity.

"We were facing the lake — a shining expanse of silver radiation, its surface shifting and crawling, as though a great undulating blanket of silver mist lay upon it. And coming down to meet it from the sky were innumerable lines of silver — a vast curtain of silver cords that broke apart into great strings of pearls when I followed their downward course.

"And then, as I turned to Lylda, I was struck with the extraordinary weirdness of her beauty as never before. The reflected light from the rain had something the quality of our moonlight. Shining on Lylda's body, it tremendously enhanced the iridescence of her skin. And her face, upturned to mine, bore an expression of radiant happiness and peace such as I had never seen before on a woman's countenance."

The Chemist paused, his voice dying away into silence as he sat lost in thought. Then he pulled himself together with a start. "It was a sight, gentlemen, the memory of which I shall cherish all my life.

"The next day was that set for my entrance into the war. Lylda and I had talked nearly all night, and had decided that she was to return with me to my world. By morning the rain had stopped, and we sat together in the window-opening,

silenced with the thrill of the wonderful new joy that had come into our hearts.

"The country before us, under the cloudless, starry sky, stretched gray-blue and beautiful into the quivering obscurity of the distance. At our feet lay the city, just awakening into life. Beyond, over the rolling meadows and fields, wound the road that led out to the battle-front, and coming back over it now, we could see an endless line of vehicles. These, as they passed through the street beneath our window, I found were loaded with soldiers, wounded and dying. I shuddered at the sight of one cart in particular, and Lylda pressed close to me, pleading with her eyes for my help for her stricken people.

"My exit from the castle was made quite a ceremony. A band of music and a guard of several hundred soldiers ushered me forth, walking beside the king, with Lylda a few paces behind. As we passed through the streets of the city, heading for the open country beyond, we were cheered continually by the people who thronged the streets and crowded upon the housetops to watch us pass.

"Outside Arite I was taken perhaps a mile, where a wide stretch of country gave me the necessary space for my growth. We were standing upon a slight hill, below which, in a vast semicircle, fully a hundred thousand people were watching.

"And now, for the first time, fear overcame me. I realized my situation — saw myself in a detached sort of way — a stranger in this extraordinary world, and only the power of my drug to raise me out of it. This drug you must remember, I had not as yet taken. Suppose it were not to act? Or were to act wrongly?

"I glanced around. The king stood before me, quietly waiting my pleasure. Then I turned to Lylda. One glance at her proud, happy little face, and my fear left me as suddenly as it had come. I took her in my arms and kissed her, there before that multitude. Then I set her down, and signified to the king I was ready.

"I took a minute quantity of one of the drugs, and as I had done before, sat down with my eyes covered. My sensations were fairly similar to those I have already described. When I looked up after a moment, I found the landscape dwindling to tiny proportions in quite as astonishing a way as it had grown before. The king and Lylda stood now hardly above my ankle.

"A great cry arose from the people — a cry wherein horror, fear, and applause seemed equally mixed. I looked down and saw thousands of them running away in terror.

"Still smaller grew everything within my vision, and then, after a moment, the landscape seemed at rest. I kneeled now upon the ground, carefully, to avoid treading on any of the people around me. I located Lylda and the king after a moment; tiny little creatures less than an inch in height. I was then, I estimated, from their viewpoint, about four hundred feet tall.

"I put my hand flat upon the ground near Lylda, and after a moment she climbed into it, two soldiers lifting her up the side of my thumb as it lay upon the ground. In the hollow of my palm, she lay quite securely, and very carefully I raised her up towards my face. Then, seeing that she was frightened, I set her down again.

"At my feet, hardly more than a few steps away, lay the tiny city of Arite and the lake. I could see all around the latter now, and could make out clearly a line of hills on the other side. Off to the left the road wound up out of sight in the distance. As far as I could see, a line of soldiers was passing out along this road — marching four abreast, with carts at intervals, loaded evidently with supplies; only occasionally, now, vehicles passed in the other direction. Can I make it plain to you, gentlemen, my sensations in changing stature? I felt at first as though I were tremendously high in the air, looking down as from a balloon upon the familiar territory beneath me. That feeling passed after a few moments, and I found that my point of view had changed. I no longer felt that I was looking down from a balloon, but felt as a normal person feels. And again I conceived myself but six feet tall, standing above a dainty little toy world. It is all in the viewpoint, of course, and never, during all my changes, was I for more than a moment able to feel of a different stature than I am at this present instant. It was always everything else that changed.

"According to the directions I had received from the king, I started now to follow the course of the road. I found it difficult walking, for the country was dotted with houses, trees, and cultivated fields, and each footstep was a separate problem.

"I progressed in this manner perhaps two miles, covering what the day

before I would have called about a hundred and thirty or forty miles.

The country became wilder as I advanced, and now was in places crowded with separate collections of troops.

"I have not mentioned the commotion I made in this walk over the country. My coming must have been told widely by couriers the night before, to soldiers and peasantry alike, or the sight of me would have caused utter demoralization. As it was, I must have been terrifying to a tremendous degree. I think the careful way in which I picked my course, stepping in the open as much as possible, helped to reassure the people. Behind me, whenever I turned, they seemed rather more curious than fearful, and once or twice when I stopped for a few moments they approached my feet closely. One athletic young soldier caught the loose end of the string of one of my buskins, as it hung over my instep close to the ground and pulled himself up hand over hand, amid the enthusiastic cheers of his comrades.

"I had walked nearly another

mile, when almost in front of me, and perhaps a hundred yards away, I saw a remarkable sight that I did not at first understand. The country here was crossed by a winding river running in a general way at right angles to my line of progress. At the right, near at hand, and on the nearer bank of the river, lay a little city, perhaps half the size of Arite, with its back up against a hill.

"What first attracted my attention was that from a dark patch across the river which seemed to be woods, pebbles appeared to pop up at intervals, traversing a little arc perhaps as high as my knees, and falling into the city. I watched for a moment and then I understood. There was a siege in progress, and the catapults of the Malites were bombarding the city with rocks.

"I went up a few steps closer, and the pebbles stopped coming. I stood now beside the city, and as I bent over it, I could see by the battered houses the havoc the bombardment had caused. Inert little figures lay in the streets, and I bent lower and inserted my thumb and forefinger between a row of houses and picked one up. It was the body of a woman, partly mashed. I set it down again hastily.

"Then as I stood up, I felt a sting on my leg. A pebble had hit me on the shin and dropped at my feet. I picked it up. It was the size of a small walnut — a huge bowlder six feet or more in diameter it would have been in Lylda's eyes. At the thought of her I was struck with a sudden fit of anger. I flung the pebble violently down into the wooded patch and leaped over the river in one bound, landing squarely on both feet in the woods. It was like jumping into a patch of ferns.

"I stamped about me for a moment until a large part of the woods was crushed down. Then I bent over and poked around with my finger.

Underneath the tangled wreckage of tiny-tree trunks, lay numbers of the Malites. I must have trodden upon a thousand or more, as one would stamp upon insects.

"The sight sickened me at first, for after all, I could not look upon them as other than men, even though they were only the length of my thumb-nail. I walked a few steps forward, and in all directions I could see swarms of the little creatures running. Then the memory of my coming departure from this world with Lylda, and my promise to the king to rid his land once for all from these people, made me feel again that they, like vermin, were to be destroyed.

"Without looking directly down, I spent the next two hours stamping over this entire vicinity. Then I ran two or three miles directly toward the country of the Malites, and returning I stamped along the course of the river for a mile or so in both directions. Then I walked back to Arite, again picking my way carefully among crowds of Oroids, who now feared me so little that I had difficulty in moving without stepping upon them.

"When I had regained my former size, which needed two successive doses of the drug, I found myself surrounded by a crowd of the Oroids, pushing and shoving each other in an effort to get closer to me. The news of my success over their enemy have been divined by them, evidently. Lord knows it must have been obvious enough what I was going to do, when they saw me stride away, a being four hundred feet tall.

"Their enthusiasm and thankfulness now were so mixed with awe and reverent worship of me as a divine being, that when I advanced toward Arite they opened a path immediately. The king, accompanied by Lylda, met me at the edge of the city. The latter threw herself into my arms at once, crying with relief to find me the proper size once more.

"I need not go into details of the ceremonies of rejoicing that took place this afternoon. These people seemed little given to pomp and public demonstration. The king made a speech from his balcony, telling them all I had done, and the city was given over to festivities and preparations to receive the returning soldiers."

The Chemist pushed his chair back from the table, and moistened his dry lips with a swallow of water. "I tell you, gentlemen," he continued, "I felt pretty happy that day. It's a wonderful feeling to find yourself the savior of a nation."

At that the Doctor jumped to his feet, overturning his chair, and striking the table a blow with his fist that made the glasses dance.

"By God!" he fairly shouted, "that's just what you can be here to us."

The Banker looked startled, while the Very Young Man pulled the Chemist by the coat in his eagerness to be heard. "A few of those pills," he said in a voice that quivered with excitement, "when you are standing in France, and you can walk over to Berlin and kick the houses apart with the toe of your boot."

"Why not?" said the Big Business Man, and silence fell on the group as they stared at each other, awed by the possibilities that opened up before them.

Chapter VIII
'I Must Go Back'

The tremendous plan for the salvation of their own suffering world through the Chemist's discovery occupied the five friends for some time.

Then laying aside this subject, that now had become of the most vital importance to them all, the Chemist resumed his narrative.

"My last evening in the world of the ring, I spent with Lylda, discussing our future, and making plans for the journey. I must tell you now, gentlemen, that never for a moment during my stay in Arite was I once free from an awful dread of this return trip. I tried to conceive what it would be like, and the more I thought about it, the more hazardous it seemed.

"You must realize, when I was growing smaller, coming in, I was able to climb down, or fall or slide down, into the spaces as they

opened up. Going back, I could only imagine the world as closing in upon me, crushing me to death unless I could find a larger space immediately above into which I could climb.

"And as I talked with Lylda about this and tried to make her understand what I hardly understood myself, I gradually was brought to realize the full gravity of the danger confronting us. If only I had made the trip out once before, I could have ventured it with her. But as I looked at her fragile little body, to expose it to the terrible possibilities of such a journey was unthinkable.

"There was another question, too, that troubled me. I had been gone from you nearly a week, and you were only to wait for me two days. I believed firmly that I was living at a faster rate, and that probably my time with you had not expired. But I did not know. And suppose, when I had come out on to the surface of the ring, one of you had had it on his finger walking along the street? No, I did not want Lylda with me in that event.

"And so I told her — made her understand — that she must stay behind, and that I would come back for her. She did not protest. She said nothing — just looked up into my face with wide, staring eyes and a little quiver of her lips. Then she clutched my hand and fell into a low, sobbing cry.

"I held her in my arms for a few moments, so little, so delicate, so human in her sorrow, and yet almost superhuman in her radiant beauty. Soon she stopped crying and smiled up at me bravely.

"Next morning I left. Lylda took me through the tunnels and back into the forest by the river's edge where I had first met her. There we parted. I can see, now, her pathetic, drooping little figure as she trudged back to the tunnel.

"When she had disappeared, I sat down to plan out my journey. I resolved now to reverse as nearly as possible the steps I had taken coming in. Acting on this decision, I started back to that portion of the forest where I had trampled it down.

"I found the place without difficulty, stopping once on the way to eat a few berries, and some of the food I carried with me. Then I took a small amount of one of the drugs, and in a few moments the forest trees had dwindled into tiny twigs beneath my feet.

"I started now to find the huge incline down which I had fallen, and when I reached it, after some hours of wandering, I followed its bottom edge to where a pile of rocks and dirt marked my former landing-place. The rocks were much larger than I remembered them, and so I knew I was not so large, now, as when I was here before.

"Remembering the amount of the drug I had taken coming down, I took now twelve of the pills. Then, in a sudden panic, I hastily took two of the others. The result made my head swim most horribly. I sat or lay down, I forget which. When I looked up I saw the hills beyond the river and forest coming towards me, yet dwindling away beneath my feet as they approached. The incline seemed folding up upon itself, like a telescope. As I watched, its upper edge came into view, a curved, luminous line against the blackness above. Every instant it crawled down closer, more sharply curved, and its inclined surface grew steeper.

"All this time, as I stood still, the ground beneath my feet seemed to be moving. It was crawling towards me, and folding up underneath where I was standing. Frequently I had to move to avoid rocks that came at me and passed under my feet into nothingness.

"Then, all at once, I realized that I had been stepping constantly backward, to avoid the inclined wall as it shoved itself towards me. I turned to see what was behind, and horror made my flesh creep at what I saw. A black, forbidding wall, much like the incline in front, entirely encircled me. It was hardly more than half a mile away, and towered four or five thousand feet overhead.

"And as I stared in terror, I could see it closing in, the line of its upper edge coming steadily closer and lower. I looked wildly around with an overpowering impulse to run. In every direction towered this rocky wall, inexorably swaying in to crush me.

"I think I fainted. When I came to myself the scene had not greatly changed. I was lying at the bottom and against one wall of a circular pit, now about a thousand feet in diameter and nearly twice as deep. The wall all around I could see was almost perpendicular, and it seemed impossible to ascend its smooth, shining sides. The action of the drug had evidently worn off, for everything was quite still.

"My fear had now left me, for I remembered this circular pit quite well. I walked over to its center, and looking around and up to its top I estimated distances carefully. Then I took two more of the pills.

"Immediately the familiar, sickening, crawling sensation began again. As the walls closed in upon me, I kept carefully in the center of the pit. Steadily they crept in. Now only a few hundred feet away! Now only a few paces — and then I reached out and touched both sides at once with my hands.

"I tell you, gentlemen, it was a terrifying sensation to stand in that well (as it now seemed), and feel its walls closing up with irresistible force. But now the upper edge was within reach of my fingers. I leaped upward and hung for a moment, then pulled myself up and scrabbled out, tumbling in a heap on the ground above. As I recovered myself, I looked again at the hole out of which I had escaped; it was hardly big enough to contain my fist.

"I knew, now, I was at the bottom of the scratch. But how different it looked than before. It seemed this time a long, narrow cañon, hardly more than sixty feet across. I glanced up and saw the blue sky overhead, flooded with light, that I knew was the space of this room above the ring.

"The problem now was quite a different one than getting out of the pit, for I saw that the scratch was so deep in proportion to its width that if I let myself get too big, I would be crushed by its walls before I could jump out. It would be necessary, therefore, to stay comparatively small and climb up its side.

"I selected what appeared to be an especially rough section, and took a portion of another of the pills. Then I started to climb. After an hour the buskins on my feet were torn to fragments, and I was bruised and battered as you saw me. I see, now, how I could have made both the descent into the ring, and my journey back with comparatively little effort, but I did the best I knew at the time.

"When the cañon was about ten feet in width, and I had been climbing arduously for several hours, I found myself hardly more than 15 or 20 feet above its bottom. And I was still almost that far from the top. With the stature I had then attained, I could have climbed the remaining distance easily, but for the fact that the wall above had grown too smooth to afford a foothold. The effects of the drug had again worn off, and I sat down and prepared to take another dose. I did so — the smallest amount I could — and held ready in my hand a pill of the other kind in case of emergency. Steadily the walls closed in.

"A terrible feeling of dizziness now came over me. I clutched the rock beside which I was sitting, and it seemed to melt like ice beneath my grasp. Then I remembered seeing the edge of the cañon within reach above my head, and with my last remaining strength, I pulled myself up, and fell upon the surface of the ring. You know the rest. I took another dose of the powder, and in a few minutes was back among you."

The Chemist stopped speaking, and looked at his friends. "Well," he said, "you've heard it all. What do you think of it?"

"It is a terrible thing to me," sighed the Very Young Man, "that you did not bring Llyda with you."

"It would have been a terrible thing if I had brought her. But I am going back for her."

"When do you plan to go back?" asked the Doctor after a moment.

"As soon as I can — in a day or two," answered the Chemist.

"Before you do your work here? You must not," remonstrated the Big Business Man. "Our war here needs you, our nation, the whole cause of liberty and freedom needs you. You cannot go."

"Lylda needs me, too," returned the Chemist. "I have an obligation towards her now, you know, quite apart from my own feelings. Understand me, gentlemen," he continued earnestly, "I do not place myself and mine before the great fight for democracy and justice being waged in this world. That would be absurd. But it is not quite that way, actually; I can go back for Lylda and return here in a week. That week will make little difference to the war. On the other hand, if I go to France first, it may take me a good many months to complete my task, and during that time Lylda will be using up her life several times faster than I. No, gentlemen, I am going to her first."

"That week you propose to take," said the Banker slowly, "will cost this world thousands of lives that you could save. Have you thought of that?"

The Chemist flushed. "I can recognize the salvation of a nation or a cause," he returned hotly, "but if I must choose between the lives of a thousand men who are not dependent on me, and the life or welfare of one woman who is, I shall choose the woman."

"He's right, you know," said the Doctor, and the Very Young Man agreed with him fervently.

Two days later the company met again in the privacy of the clubroom. When they had finished dinner, the Chemist began in his usual quiet way:

"I am going to ask you this time, gentlemen, to give me a full week. There are four of you – six hours a day of watching for each. It need not be too great a hardship. You see," he continued, as they nodded in agreement, "I want to spend a longer period in the ring world this time. I may never go back, and I want to learn, in the interest of science, as much about it as I can. I was there such a short time before, and it was all so strange and remarkable, I confess I learned practically nothing.

"I told you all I could of its history. But of its arts, its science, and all its sociological and economic questions, I got hardly more than a glimpse. It is a world and a people far less advanced than ours, yet with something we have not, and probably never will have – the universally distributed milk of human kindness. Yes, gentlemen, it is a world well worth studying."

The Banker came out of a brown study. "How about your formulas for these drugs?" he asked abruptly; "where are they?" The Chemist tapped his forehead smilingly. "Well, hadn't you better leave them with us?" the Banker pursued. "The hazards of your trip – you can't tell – – "

"Don't misunderstand me, gentlemen," broke in the Chemist. "I wouldn't give you those formulas if my life and even Lylda's depended on it. There again you do not differentiate between the individual and the race. I know you four very well. You are my friends, with all the bond that friendship implies. I believe in your integrity – each of you I trust implicitly. With these formulas you could crush Germany, or you could, any one of you, rule the world, with all its treasures for your own. These drugs are the most powerful thing for good in the world to-day. But they are equally as powerful for evil. I would stake my life on what you would do, but I will not stake the life of a nation."

"I know what I'd do if I had the formulas," began the Very Young Man.

"Yes, but I don't know what you'd do," laughed the Chemist. "Don't you see I'm right?" They admitted they did, though the Banker

acquiesced very grudgingly.

"The time of my departure is at hand. Is there anything else, gentlemen, before I leave you?" asked the Chemist, beginning to disrobe.

"Please tell Lylda I want very much to meet her," said the Very Young Man earnestly, and they all laughed.

When the room was cleared, and the handkerchief and ring in place once more, the Chemist turned to them again. "Good-by, my friends," he said, holding out his hands. "One week from to-night, at most."

Then he took the pills.

No unusual incident marked his departure. The last they saw of him he was calmly sitting on the ring near the scratch.

Then passed the slow days of watching, each taking his turn for the allotted six hours.

By the fifth day, they began to hourly expect the Chemist, but it passed through its weary length, and he did not come. The sixth day dragged by, and then came the last — the day he had promised would end their watching. Still he did not come, and in the evening they gathered, and all four watched together, each unwilling to miss the return of the adventurer and his woman from another world.

But the minutes lengthened into hours, and midnight found the white-faced little group, hopeful yet hopeless, with fear tugging at their hearts. A second week passed, and still they watched, explaining with an optimism they could none of them feel, the non-appearance of their friend. At the end of the second week they met again to talk the situation over, a dull feeling of fear and horror possessing them. The Doctor was the first to voice what now each of them was forced to believe.

"I guess it's all useless," he said. "He's not coming back."

"I don't hardly dare give him up," said the Big Business Man.

"Me, too," agreed the Very Young Man sadly.

The Doctor sat for some time in silence, thoughtfully regarding the ring. "My friends," he began finally, "this is too big a thing to deal with in any but the most careful way. I can't imagine what is going on inside that ring, but I do know what is happening in our world, and what our friend's return means to civilization here. Under the circumstances, therefore, I cannot, I will not give him up.

"I am going to put that ring in a museum and pay for having it watched indefinitely. Will you join me?"

He turned to the Big Business Man as he spoke.

"Make it a threesome," said the Banker gruffly. "What do you take me for?" and the Very Young Man sighed with the tragedy of youth.

To Be Continued...

ZIRL & SONS PUBLISHERS

The Altar at Midnight

A Classic From an Underrated Master

By C.M. Kornbluth

He had quite a rum-blossom on him for a kid, I thought at first. But when he moved closer to the light by the cash register to ask the bartender for a match or something, I saw it wasn't that. Not just the nose. Broken veins on his cheeks, too, and the funny eyes. He must have seen me look, because he slid back away from the light.

The bartender shook my bottle of ale in front of me like a Swiss bell-ringer so it foamed inside the green glass.

"You ready for another, sir?" he asked.

I shook my head. Down the bar, he tried it on the kid – he was drinking scotch and water or something like that – and found out he could push him around. He sold him three scotch and waters in 10 minutes.

When he tried for number four, the kid had his courage up and said, "I'll tell you when I'm ready for another, Jack." But there wasn't any trouble.

It was almost nine and the place began to fill up. The manager, a real hood type, stationed himself by the door to screen out the high-school kids and give the big hello to conventioneers. The girls came hurrying in, too, with their little makeup cases and their fancy hair piled up and their frozen faces with the perfect mouths drawn on them. One of them stopped to say something to the manager, some excuse about something, and he said: "That's aw ri'; get inna dressing room."

A three-piece band behind the drapes at the back of the stage began to make warm-up noises and there were two bartenders keeping busy. Mostly it was beer — a midweek crowd. I finished my ale and had to wait a couple of minutes before I could get another bottle. The bar filled up from the end near the stage because all the customers wanted a good, close look at the strippers for their 50-cent bottles of beer. But I noticed that nobody sat down next to the kid, or, if anybody did, he didn't stay long — you go out for some fun and the bartender pushes you around and nobody wants to sit next to you. I picked up my bottle and glass and went down on the stool to his left.

He turned to me right away and said: "What kind of a place is this, anyway?" The broken veins were all over his face, little ones, but so many, so close, that they made his face look something like marbled rubber. The funny look in his eyes was it — the trick contact lenses. But I tried not to stare and not to look away.

"It's OK," I said. "It's a good show if you don't mind a lot of noise from—"

He stuck a cigarette into his mouth and poked the pack at me. "I'm a spacer," he said, interrupting.

I took one of his cigarettes and said: "Oh."

He snapped a lighter for the cigarettes and said: "Venus."

I was noticing that his pack of cigarettes on the bar had some kind of yellow sticker instead of the blue tax stamp.

"Ain't that a crock?" he asked. "You can't smoke and they give you lighters for a souvenir. But it's a good lighter. On Mars last week, they gave us all some cheap pen-and-pencil sets."

"You get something every trip, hah?" I took a good, long drink of ale and he finished his scotch and water.

"Shoot. You call a trip a 'shoot.'"

One of the girls was working her way down the bar. She was going to slide onto the empty stool at his right and give him the business, but she looked at him first and decided not to. She curled around me and asked if I'd buy her a li'l ole drink. I said no and she moved on to the next. I could kind of feel the young fellow quivering. When I looked at him, he stood up. I followed him out of the dump. The manager grinned without thinking and said, "G'night, boys," to us.

The kid stopped in the street and said to me: "You don't have to follow me around, Pappy." He sounded like one wrong word and I would get socked in the teeth.

"Take it easy. I know a place where they won't spit in your eye."

He pulled himself together and made a joke of it. "This I have to see," he said. "Near here?"

"A few blocks."

We started walking. It was a nice night.

"I don't know this city at all," he said. "I'm from Covington, Kentucky. You do your drinking at home there. We don't have places like this." He meant the whole Skid Row area.

"It's not so bad," I said. "I spend a lot of time here."

"Is that a fact? I mean, down home a man your age would likely have a wife and children."

"I do. The hell with them."

He laughed like a real youngster and I figured he couldn't even be 25. He didn't have any trouble with the broken curbstones in spite of his scotch and waters. I asked him about it.

"Sense of balance," he said. "You have to be tops for balance to be a spacer — you spend so much time outside in a suit. People don't know how much. Punctures. And you aren't worth a damn if you lose your point."

"What's that mean?"

"Oh. Well, it's hard to describe. When you're outside and you lose your point, it means you're all mixed up, you don't know which way the can — that's the ship — which way the can is. It's having all that room around you. But if you have a good balance, you feel a little tugging to the ship, or maybe you just know which way the ship is without feeling it. Then you have your point and you can get the work done."

"There must be a lot that's hard to describe."

He thought that might be a crack and he clammed up on me.

"You call this Gandytown," I said after a while. "It's where the stove-up old railroad men hang out. This is the place."

It was the second week of the month, before everybody's pension check was all gone. Oswiak's was jumping. The Grandsons of the Pioneers were on the juke singing the Man from Mars Yodel and old Paddy Shea was jigging in the middle of the floor. He had a full seidel of beer in his right hand and his empty left sleeve was flapping.

The kid balked at the screen door. "Too damn bright," he said.

I shrugged and went on in and he followed. We sat down at a table. At Oswiak's you can drink at the bar if you want to, but none of the regulars do.

Paddy jigged over and said: "Welcome home, Doc." He's a Liverpool Irishman; they talk like Scots, some say, but they sound almost like Brooklyn to me.

"Hello, Paddy. I brought somebody uglier than you. Now what do you say?"

Paddy jigged around the kid in a half-circle with his sleeve flapping and then flopped into a chair when the record stopped. He took a big drink from the seidel and said: "Can he do this?" Paddy stretched his face into an awful grin that showed his teeth. He has three of them. The kid laughed and asked me: "What the hell did you drag me into here for?"

"Paddy says he'll buy drinks for the house the day anybody uglier than he is comes in."

Oswiak's wife waddled over for the order and the kid asked us

what we'd have. I figured I could start drinking, so it was three double scotches.

After the second round, Paddy started blowing about how they took his arm off without any anesthetics except a bottle of gin because the red-ball freight he was tangled up in couldn't wait.

That brought some of the other old gimps over to the table with their stories.

Blackie Bauer had been sitting in a boxcar with his legs sticking through the door when the train started with a jerk. Wham, the door closed. Everybody laughed at Blackie for being that dumb in the first place, and he got mad.

Sam Fireman has palsy. This week he was claiming he used to be a watchmaker before he began to shake. The week before, he'd said he was a brain surgeon. A woman I didn't know, a real old Boxcar Bertha, dragged herself over and began some kind of story about how her sister married a Greek, but she passed out before we found out what happened.

Somebody wanted to know what was wrong with the kid's face — Bauer, I think it was, after he came back to the table.

"Compression and decompression," the kid said. "You're all the time climbing into your suit and out of your suit. Inboard air's thin to start with. You get a few redlines — that's these ruptured blood vessels — and you say the hell with the money; all you'll make is just one more trip. But, God, it's a lot of money for anybody my age! You keep saying that until you can't be anything but a spacer. The eyes are hard-radiation scars."

"You like dot all ofer?" asked Oswiak's wife politely.

"All over, ma'am," the kid told her in a miserable voice. "But I'm going to quit before I get a Bowman Head."

"I don't care," said Maggie Rorty. "I think he's cute."

"Compared with—" Paddy began, but I kicked him under the table.

We sang for a while, and then we told gags and recited limericks for a while, and I noticed that the kid and Maggie had wandered into the back room — the one with the latch on the door.

Oswiak's wife asked me, very puzzled: "Doc, w'y dey do dot flyink by planyets?"

"It's the damn govermint," Sam Fireman said.

"Why not?" I said. "They got the Bowman Drive, why the hell shouldn't they use it? Serves 'em right." I had a double scotch and added: "Twenty years of it and they found out a few things they didn't know. Redlines are only one of them. Twenty years more, maybe they'll find out a few more things they didn't know. Maybe by the time there's a bathtub in every American home and an alcoholism clinic in every American town, they'll find out a whole lot of things they didn't know. And every American boy will be a popeyed, blood-raddled wreck, like our friend here, from riding the

Bowman Drive."

"It's the damn govermint," Sam Fireman repeated.

"And what the hell did you mean by that remark about alcoholism?" Paddy said, real sore. "Personally, I can take it or leave it alone."

So we got to talking about that and everybody there turned out to be people who could take it or leave it alone.

It was maybe midnight when the kid showed at the table again, looking kind of dazed. I was drunker than I ought to be by midnight, so I said I was going for a walk. He tagged along and we wound up on a bench at Screwball Square. The soap-boxers were still going strong. Like I said, it was a nice night. After a while, a pot-bellied old auntie who didn't give a damn about the face sat down and tried to talk the kid into going to see some etchings. The kid didn't get it and I led him over to hear the soap-boxers before there was trouble.

One of the orators was a mush-mouthed evangelist. "And, oh, my friends," he said, "when I looked through the porthole of the spaceship and beheld the wonder of the Firmament—"

"You're a stinkin' Yankee liar!" the kid yelled at him. "You say one damn more word about can-shootin' and I'll ram your spaceship down your lyin' throat! Wheah's your redlines if you're such a hot spacer?"

The crowd didn't know what he was talking about, but "wheah's your redlines" sounded good to them, so they heckled mush-mouth off his box with it.

I got the kid to a bench. The liquor was working in him all of a sudden. He simmered down after a while and asked: "Doc, should I've given Miz Rorty some money? I asked her afterward and she said she'd admire to have something to remember me by, so I gave her my lighter. She seem' to be real pleased with it. But I was wondering if maybe I embarrassed her by asking her right out. Like I tol' you, back in Covington, Kentucky, we don't have places like that. Or maybe we did and I just didn't know about them. But what do you think I should've done about Miz Rorty?"

"Just what you did," I told him. "If they want money, they ask you for it first. Where you staying?"

"Y.M.C.A.," he said, almost asleep. "Back in Covington, Kentucky, I was a member of the Y and I kept up my membership. They have to let me in because I'm a member. Spacers have all kinds of trouble, Doc. Woman trouble. Hotel trouble. Fam'ly trouble. Religious trouble. I was raised a Southern Baptist, but wheah's Heaven, anyway? I ask' Doctor Chitwood las' time home before the redlines got so thick — Doc, you aren't a minister of the Gospel, are you? I hope I di'n' say anything to offend you."

"No offense, son," I said. "No offense."

I walked him to the avenue and

waited for a fleet cab. It was almost five minutes. The independents that roll drunks dent the fenders of fleet cabs if they show up in Skid Row and then the fleet drivers have to make reports on their own time to the company. It keeps them away. But I got one and dumped the kid in.

"The Y Hotel," I told the driver. "Here's five. Help him in when you get there."

When I walked through Screwball Square again, some college kids were yelling "wheah's your redlines" at old Charlie, the last of the Wobblies.

Old Charlie kept roaring: "The hell with your breadlines! I'm talking about atomic bombs. Right — up — there!" And he pointed at the Moon.

It was a nice night, but the liquor was dying in me.

There was a joint around the corner, so I went in and had a drink to carry me to the club; I had a bottle there. I got into the first cab that came.

"Athletic Club," I said.

"Inna dawghouse, harh?" the driver said, and he gave me a big personality smile.

I didn't say anything and he started the car.

He was right, of course. I was in everybody's doghouse. Some day I'd scare hell out of Tom and Lise by going home and showing them what their daddy looked like.

Down at the Institute, I was in the doghouse.

"Oh, dear," everybody at the Institute said to everybody, "I'm sure I don't know what ails the man. A lovely wife and two lovely grown children and she had to tell him 'either you go or I go.' And drinking! And this is rather subtle, but it's a well-known fact that neurotics seek out low company to compensate for their guilt-feelings. The places he frequents. Doctor Francis Bowman, the man who made space-flight a reality. The man who put the Bomb Base on the Moon! Really, I'm sure I don't know what ails him."

The hell with them all.

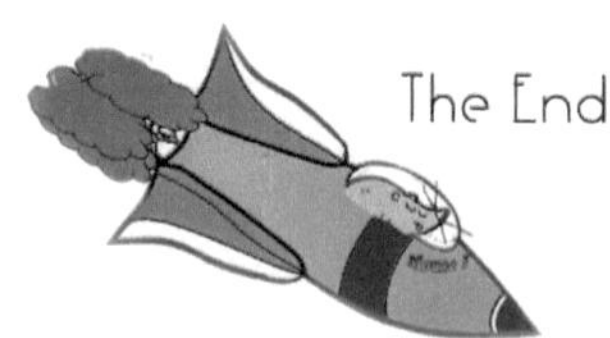

Through the Gates of the Silver Key

continued from page 51

of years of time, and uncounted billions of miles that Randolph Carter hurtled through space as a nameless, alien entity in a thin envelope of electron-activated metal. He timed his period of suspended animation with utmost care, planning to have it end only a few years before the time of landing on the Earth in or near 1928.

"He will never forget that awakening. Remember, gentlemen, that before that eon long sleep he had lived consciously for thousands of terrestrial years amidst the alien and horrible wonders of Yaddith. There was a hideous gnawing of cold, a cessation of menacing dreams, and a glance through the eye-plates of the envelope. Stars, clusters, nebulae, on every hand - and at last their outline bore some kinship to the constellations of Earth that he knew.

"Some day his descent into the solar system may be told. He saw Kynath and Yuggoth on the rim, passed close to Neptune and glimpsed the hellish white fungi that spot it, learned an untellable secret from the close glimpsed mists of Jupiter, and saw the horror on one of the satellites, and gazed at the cyclopean ruins that sprawl over Mars' ruddy disc. When the Earth drew near he saw it as a thin crescent which swelled alarmingly in size. He slackened speed, though his sensations of homecoming made him wish to lose not a moment. I will not try to tell you of these sensations as I learned them from Carter.

"Well, toward the last Carter hovered about in the Earth's upper air waiting till daylight came over the Western Hemisphere. He wanted to land where he had left - near the Snake Den in the hills behind Arkham. If any of you have been away from home long - and I know one of you has - I leave it to you how the sight of New England's rolling hills and great elms and gnarled orchards and ancient stone walls must have affected him.

"He came down at dawn in the lower meadow of the old Carter place, and was thankful for the silence and solitude. It was autumn, as when he had left, and the smell of the hills was balm to his soul. He managed to drag the metal envelope up the slope of the timber lot into the Snake Den, though it would not go through the weed-choked fissure to the inner cave. It was there also that he covered his alien body with the human clothing and waxen mask which would be necessary. He kept the envelope here for over a year, till certain circumstances made a new hiding-place necessary.

"He walked to Arkham - incidentally practicing the management of his body in human posture and against terrestrial gravity - and his gold changed to money at a bank. He also made some inquiries - posing as a foreigner ignorant of much English - and found that the year was 1930, only two years after the goal he had aimed at.

"Of course, his position was horrible. Unable to assert his identity, forced to live on guard every moment, with certain difficulties regarding food, and with a need to conserve the alien drug which kept his Zkauba-facet dormant, he felt that he must act as quickly as possible. Going to Boston and taking a room in the decaying West End, where he could live cheaply and inconspicuously, he at once established inquiries concerning Randolph Carter's estate and effects. It was then that he learned how anxious Mr. Aspinwall, here, was to have the estate divided, and how valiantly Mr. de Marigny and Mr. Phillips strove to keep it intact."

The Hindoo bowed, though no expression crossed his dark, tranquil, and thickly bearded face.

"Indirectly," he continued, "Carter secured a good copy of the missing parchment and began working on its deciphering. I am glad to say that I was able to help in all this - for he appealed to me quite early, and through me came in touch with other mystics throughout the world. I went to live with him in Boston - a wretched place in Chambers Street. As for the parchment - I am pleased to help Mr. de Marigny in his perplexity. To him let me say that the language of those hieroglyphics is not Naacal, but R'lyehian, which was brought to Earth by the spawn of Cthulhu countless ages ago. It is, of course, a translation - there was an Hyperborean original millions of years earlier in the primal tongue of Tsath-yo.

"There was more to decipher than Carter had looked for, but at no time did he give up hope. Early this year he made great strides through a book he imported from Nepal, and there is no question but that he will win before long. Unfortunately, however, one handicap has developed - the exhaustion of the alien drug which keeps the Zkauba-facet dormant. This is not, however, as great a calamity as was feared. Carter's personality is gaining in the body, and when Zkauba comes upper most - for shorter and shorter periods, and now only when evoked by some unusual excitement - he is generally too dazed to undo any of Carter's work. He can not find the metal envelope that would take him back to Yaddith, for although he almost did, once, Carter hid it anew at a time when the Zkanba-facet was wholly latent. All the harm he has done is to frighten a few people and create certain nightmare rumors among the Poles and Lithuanians of Boston's West End. So far, he had never injured the careful disguise prepared by the Carter-facet, though he sometimes throws it off so that parts have to be replaced. I have seen what lies beneath - and it is not good to see.

"A month ago Carter saw the advertisement of this meeting, and knew that he must act quickly to save his estate. He could not wait to decipher the parchment and resume his human form. Consequently he deputed me to act for him.

"Gentlemen, I say to you that Randolph Carter is not dead; that he is temporarily in an anomalous condition, but that within two or three months at the outside he will be able to appear in proper form and demand the custody of his estate. I am prepared to offer proof if necessary. Therefore I beg that you will adjourn this meeting for an indefinite period."

Chapter Eight

De Marigny and Phillips stared at the Hindoo as if hypnotized, while Aspinwall emitted a series of snorts and bellows. The old attorney's disgust had by now surged into open rage and he pounded the table with an apoplectically veined fit. When he spoke, it was in a kind of bark.

"How long is this foolery to be borne? I've listened an hour to this madman - this faker - and now he has the damned effrontery to say Randolph Carter is alive - to ask us to postpone the settlement for no good reason! Why don't you throw the scoundrel out, de Marigny? Do you mean to make us all the butts of a charlatan or idiot?"

De Marigny quietly raised his hand and spoke softly.

"Let us think slowly and dearly. This has been a very singular tale, and there are things in it which I, as a mystic not altogether ignorant, recognize as far from impossible. Furthermore - since 1930 I have received letters from the Swami which tally with his account."

As he paused, old Mr. Phillips ventured a word.

"Swami Chandraputra spoke of proofs. I, too, recognize much that is significant in this story, and I have myself had many oddly corroborative letters from the Swami during the last two years; but some of these statements are very extreme. Is there not something tangible which can be shown?"

At last the impassive-faced Swami replied, slowly and hoarsely, and drawing an object from the pocket of his loose coat as he spoke.

"While none of you here has ever seen the silver key itself, Messrs. de Marigny and Phillips have seen photographs of it. Does this look familiar to you?"

He fumblingly laid on the table, with his large, white-mittened hand, a heavy key of tarnished silver - nearly five inches long, of unknown and utterly exotic

workmanship, and covered from end to end with hieroglyphs of the most bizarre description. De Marigny and Phillips gasped.

"That's it!" cried de Marigny. "The camera doesn't lie I couldn't be mistaken!"

But Aspinwall had already launched a reply.

"Fools! What does it prove? If that's really the key that belonged to my cousin, it's up to this foreigner - this damned nigger - to explain how he got it! Randolph Carter vanished with the key four years ago. How do we know he wasn't robbed and murdered? He was half crazy himself, and in touch with still crazier people.

"Look here, you nigger - where did you get that key? Did you kill Randolph Carter?"

The Swami's features, abnormally placid, did not change; but the remote, irisless black eyes behind them blazed dangerously. He spoke with great difficulty.

"Please control yourself, Mr. Aspinwall. There is another form of poof that I could give, but its effect upon everybody would not be pleasant. Let us be reasonable. Here are some papers obviously written since 1930, and in the unmistakable style of Randolph Carter."

He clumsily drew a long envelope from inside his loose coat and handed it to the sputtering attorney as de Marigny and Phillips watched with chaotic thoughts and a dawning feeling of supernal wonder.

"Of course the handwriting is almost illegible - but remember that Randolph Carter now has no hands well adapted to forming human script."

Aspinwall looked through the papers hurriedly, and was visibly perplexed, but he did not change his demeanor. The room was tense with excitement and nameless dread and the alien rhythm of the coffin-shaped clock had an utterly diabolic sound to de Marigny and Phillips, though the lawyer seemed affected not at all.

Aspinwall spoke again. "These look like clever forgeries. If they aren't, they may mean that Randolph Carter has been brought under the control of people with no good purpose. There's only one thing to do - have this faker arrested. De Marigny, will you telephone for the police?"

"Let us wait," answered their host. "I do not think this case calls for the police. I have a certain idea. Mr. Aspinwall, this gentleman is a mystic of real attainments. He says he is in the confidence of Randolph Carter. Will it satisfy you if he can answer certain questions which could be answered only by one in such confidence? I know Carter, and can ask such questions. Let me get a book which I think will make a good test."

He turned toward the door to the library, Phillips dazedly following in a kind of automatic way. Aspinwall remained where he was, studying closely the Hindoo who confronted him with abnormally impassive face. Suddenly, as Chandraputra clumsily restored the silver key to his pocket the lawyer emitted a guttural shout.

"Hey, by Heaven I've got it! This rascal is in disguise. I don't believe he's an East Indian at all. That face - it isn't a face, but a mask! I guess his story put that into my head, but it's true. It never moves, and that turban and beard hide the edges. This fellow's a common crook! He isn't even a foreigner - I've been watching his language. He's a Yankee of some sort. And look at those mittens - he knows his fingerprints could be spotted. Damn you, I'll pull that thing off -"

"Stop!" The hoarse, oddly alien voice of the Swami held a tone beyond all mere earthly fright. "I told you there was another form of proof which I could give if necessary, and I warned you not to provoke me to it. This red-faced old meddler is right; I'm not really an East Indian. This face is a mask, and what it covers is not human. You others have guessed - I felt that minutes ago. It wouldn't be pleasant if I took that mask off - let it alone. Ernest, I may as well tell you that I am Randolph Carter."

No one moved. Aspinwall snorted and made vague motions. De Marigny and Phillips, across the room, watched the workings of the red face and studied the back of the turbaned figure that confronted him. The clock's abnormal ticking was hideous and the tripod fumes and swaying arras danced a dance of death. The half-choking lawyer broke the silence.

"No you don't, you crook - you can't scare me! You've reasons of your own for not wanting that mask off. Maybe we'd know who you are. Off with it -"

As he reached forward, the Swami seized his hand with one of his own clumsily mittened members, evoking a curious cry of mixed pain and surprise. De Marigny started toward the two, but paused confused as the pseudo-Hindoo's shout of protest changed to a wholly inexplicable rattling and buzzing sound. Aspinwall's red face was furious, and with his free hand he made another lunge at his opponent's bushy beard. This time he succeeded in getting a hold, and at his frantic tug the whole waxen visage came loose from the turban and clung to the lawyer's apoplectic fist.

As it did so, Aspinwall uttered a frightful gurgling cry, and Phillips and de Marigny saw his face convulsed with a wilder, deep and more hideous epilepsy of stark panic than ever they had seen on human countenance before. The pseudo-Swami had meanwhile released his other hand and was standing as if dazed, making buzzing noises of a most abnormal quality. Then the turbaned figure slumped oddly into a posture scarcely human, and began a curious, fascinated sort of shuffle toward the coffin-shaped clock that ticked out its cosmic and abnormal rhythm. His now uncovered face was turned away, and de Marigny and Phillips could not see what the lawyer's act had disclosed. Then their attention was turned to Aspinwall, who was sinking ponderously to the floor. The spell was broken-but when they reached the old man he was dead.

Turning quickly to the shuffling Swami's receding back, de Marigny saw one of the great white mittens drop listlessly off a dangling arm. The fumes of the olibanum were thick, and all that could be glimpsed of the revealed hand was something long and black... Before the Creole could reach the retreating figure, old Mr. Phillips laid a hand on his shoulder.

"Don't!" he whispered, "We don't know what we're up against. That other facet, you know - Zkauba, the wizard of Yaddith... "

The turbaned figure had now reached the abnormal clock, and the watchers saw though the dense fumes a blurred black claw fumbling with the tall, hieroglyphed door. The fumbling made a queer, clicking sound. Then the figure entered the coffin-shaped case and pulled the door shut after it.

De Marigny could no longer be restrained, but when he reached and opened the clock it was empty. The abnormal ticking went on, beating out the dark, cosmic rhythm which underlies all mystical gate-openings. On the floor the great white mitten, and the dead man with a bearded mask clutched in his hand, had nothing further to reveal.

* * * * *

A year passed, and nothing has been heard of Randolph Carter. His estate is still unsettled. The Boston address from which one "Swami Chandraputra" sent inquiries to various mystics in 1930-31-32 was indeed tenanted by a strange Hindoo, but he left shortly before the date of the New Orleans conference and has never been seen since. He was said to be dark, expressionless, and bearded, and his landlord thinks the swarthy mask - which was duly exhibited - looked very much like him. He was never, however, suspected of any connection with the nightmare apparitions whispered of by local Slavs. The hills behind Arkham were searched for the "metal envelope," but nothing of the sort was ever found. However, a clerk in Arkham's First National Bank does recall a queer turbaned man who cashed an odd bit of gold bullion in October, 1930.

De Marigny and Phillips scarcely know what to make of the business. After all, what was proved?

There was a story. There was a key which might have been forged from one of the pictures Carter had freely distributed in 1928. There were papers - all indecisive. There was a masked stranger, but who now living saw behind the mask? Amidst the strain and the olibanum fumes that act of vanishing in the clock might easily have been a dual hallucination.

Hindoos know much of hypnotism. Reason proclaims the "Swami" a criminal with designs on Randolph Carter's estate. But the autopsy said that Aspinwall had died of shock. Was it rage alone which caused it? And some things in that story...

In a vast room hung with strangely figured arras and filled with olibanum fumes, Etienne Laurent de Marigny often sits listening with vague sensations to the abnormal rhythm of that hieroglyphed, coffin-shaped clock.

Zeiss Ikon Contax

Price List No. 10

Effective Sept. 15, 1936

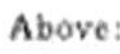

Above:
Contax I (black)

Right:
Contax II (chrome)

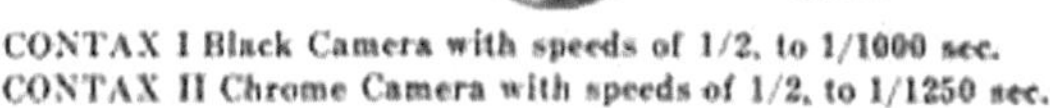

CONTAX I Black Camera with speeds of 1/2, to 1/1000 sec.
CONTAX II Chrome Camera with speeds of 1/2, to 1/1250 sec.

(prices include cable release, film spool, one magazine in container, lens cap and neckstrap)

	I BLACK	II CHROME
Camera only, without lens or lens cap	$117.00	$161.00
With Carl Zeiss Tessar F/3.5, 50 mm	174.00	218.00
With Carl Zeiss Tessar F/2.8, 50 mm	184.50	228.50
With Carl Zeiss Sonnar F/2, 50 mm	231.00	275.00
With Carl Zeiss Sonnar F/1.5, 50 mm	329.00	373.00

NOTE:—Contax cameras are not supplied without lenses.

PHENOMENAL STORIES

ZIRL & SONS PUBLISHERS

God Editor of Doom's Note: Occasionally over my years in newspapers, I got the chance to write about science fiction, horror, etc. Most of these themes appeared in one of the incarnations of my column, ***Hitchhiker in Time****. These will be reprinted here as space allows.*

Is There?

By Shawn M. Tomlinson

All day Wednesday I kept hearing David Bowie in my head.

He kept singing over and over again: "Is there life on Mars?"

See, that's the day the universe — our universe — really did change. Like everything else, though, who knows if it's real or if it's true or exactly how things will change.

It was late Tuesday, maybe early Wednesday, when the people at NASA said they found life on Mars... well, on a bit of Mars here on Earth... well, maybe "life" ... or, well maybe ancient life...

Confused? Me too

The absolute best thing about this possible discovery of life from Mars is: it came to Earth exactly the same way H.G. Wells — and later Orson Welles — said it would in *War of the Worlds*. It came on a meteor.

The NASA scientists said they found sub-microscopic fossilized microbes from something like 4.5 billion years ago. The scientific paper on the subject will come out in about 10 days, they said, but in the meantime, the NASA people did a news conference talking about it. Like typical lecturers, they showed slides.

Now a lot of people would say: "Who cares?" Those people, well, they said we didn't get anything out of the whole space program, too. Yet they live with pacemakers, advanced medicines and miniaturization daily, couldn't — probably — get by without it.

Then there are the rest of us, those of us who would answer the question "is there life elsewhere than on the Earth?" with a resounding "of course," just as a simple statement.

Hey, now look, let's set some things straight here:

I am not a UFOologist or any such thing. It's just ridiculous to think life only evolved here.

NASA scientists said they found "organic material" that could be the residuals of life because, well, hell, it looks a lot like stuff they found here.

An extremely dull lecturer from UCLA named something Schopf refuted the idea that it is life because the same kinds of material have been found in cosmic dust (Whoa, dude? What kind of dust?) previously.

The controversy over this discovery will go on for a long time.

Even if it isn't — or wasn't — life, that changes very little because we will find it someday.

I doubt very much that some people would believe other races aside from the human race exist, even if a 10-armed, 40-eyed, soft-spoken diplomat from Tau Ceti drives up in a Rolls Royce and asks Newt Gingrich if he has any Grey Poupon.

The truth is: it does matter. It matters for many, many reasons. Like, for example, the fact that the supposed fossilized remains pre-date the earliest life found on Earth by something like a billion years.

That means, according to NASA Scientist Wes Huntress, that life originated — possibly — somewhere other than on Earth. Think of the implications — theologically, egocentrically, biologically. As Professor Richard Zare of Stanford University said, we all may be Martians.

That statement itself is chilling, reminiscent of the ending of Ray Bradbury's episodic *The Martian Chronicles*, but it a much more real sense than in literature.

And *The Martian Chronicles* is literature, even if it isn't real science fiction or very plausible. There were others who once swept their imaginations across space, across the ancient Martian landscape to bring us tales.

I thought this week that it was odd that with probably the most momentous announcement in the history of the planet Earth, few of those Old Masters of science fiction who conceived the ideas, were around to share in the moment. Robert A. Heinlein, who wrote one of my favorite novels (*Double Star*, about Mars), is dead, as are Isaac Asimov, John W. Campbell Jr., H.G. Wells and the rest.

The only one left, the only one still out there is Arthur C. Clarke, but he was nowhere to be seen Wednesday, the day of the news conference. Which was odd because Clarke became world famous when he commented "live" on several of the Apollo missions for television.

Who are we?

See, in the early days of science fiction, Mars frequently was used in plot-lines as an older culture, a place where life had existed before it did here. Sometimes it still existed at the time humans got to Mars — as in the science fantasy of Edgar Rice Burroughs and the classic science fiction story "A Martian Odyssey" by Stanley G. Weinbaum. In other tales, the culture had long since died or left the planet, either for outer regions or, perhaps, for the "green hills of Earth," as Heinlein put it, long before our history. In others still — *The Martian Chronicles* by Bradbury, for example, our arrival on Mars meant the end of their civilization.

Those ideas were written off as "quaint" some time ago, as science began to say there were no "canals" on Mars as was once thought in the late 19th and early 20th centuries. Many writers abandoned Mars after the heyday of the 1930s. Perhaps now, they will have to re-think it.

Or, perhaps, I will. I'm always "in the middle of" writing a novel.

Maybe this will be the one I finish. I'll call it simply:

'Is There... ?'

112 H.P. AMERICA'S MOST POWERFUL MOTOR CAR

With the new 112 h. p. Imperial "80" Chrysler now introduces into the field of finest motor cars a new modern note of simple excellence.

Powerful, graceful and fleet, this newest Chrysler emphasizes efficient simplicity in engine and chassis, and the charm of simple good taste in body and lines.

The new 112 h.p. "Red-Head" high-compression rubber-mounted engine—a marvel of clean design—is smooth and alert, easy to drive, maintain or control. No less powerful car can approach its flawless performance.

Graceful lines and luxurious custom bodies contribute importantly to Imperial "80" pre-eminence. In their simplicity of design and correctness of good taste there is not even a hint of that over-ornamentation sometimes mistaken for smartness.

Custom bodies are built by Locke, LeBaron, Dietrich, and by Chrysler in a special plant, acquired and equipped solely to produce these fine examples of coachwork.

Five body styles—Roadster, Town Sedan, 5-passenger Sedan, 7-passenger Sedan, Sedan Limousine—$2795 to $3455. Also in custom-built types by Chrysler, Dietrich, Locke and Le Baron, up to $6795. All prices f.o.b. Detroit, subject to current Federal excise tax. Chrysler dealers are in position to extend the convenience of time payments.

CHRYSLER

IMPERIAL "80"

www.ingramcontent.com/pod-product-compliance
Ingram Content Group UK Ltd.
Pitfield, Milton Keynes, MK11 3LW, UK
UKHW041942190726
13854UKWH00004B/1739

9 780359 940417